FIRE AND ICE
By
Margaret Afseth

ISBN: 978-1-927828-48-9

Publisher's note: This novel is a work of fiction. Names, characters, places and incidents are either products of the author's imagination or used fictitiously. All characters are fictional, and similarity to people living or dead purely coincidental.

This book is dedicated to my two caring daughters: the one who is my chauffer, even when, after a hard day of work, she herself is beyond exhaustion. The other, so busy, yet she takes time to plan my covers, up load for me, and monitor my site. Without them, I would not be a published author, especially since the damage to my sight. Thank you, my sacrificial girls.

TABLE OF CONTENTS

PROLOGUE:

Three tiny treasures,
Fragile new life;
Two golden brown;
The last blue as ice.

First one orphaned,
Second forcibly taken;
Third scarcely living,
But none forsaken.

Two speak as one,
Mind words too fast;
First understands not,
Yet has knowledge from the past.

Bring these together,
Whether sister or not,
Seeking a weapon?
Beware! Better not!

Chapter 1

Brad was not going to grieve; he simply was too angry! She should not have died like that! She had cancer...brain cancer! She wasn't supposed to drowned, especially not way out in some ocean.

What was the plane doing in the Bermuda Triangle, anyway? That is nowhere near the coast of Canada where they were supposed to be heading.

But that was where they had just recently found the empty shell of the plane...at the bottom of the ocean, on the opposite side of the world.

And now, he was in a grave yard, with his motherless daughter, burying an empty box in a tiny square hole in the ground...so they could finally, have a place to bring flowers...and mourn.

They would place a slab of concrete over the hole, a marker that read with her name, and call it her grave, but...

No way! I won't believe she's dead, until I see her body! And...I'll go to the bottom of that ocean to find it, if I have to...whether it takes me the rest of my life, or not! I won't come back until I can bring her home with me!

****

All her life, Willow had heard of nothing but the 'mission'. Her daddy was obsessed by it. He meant to find the body of her mother, and bring it home.

He told stories of how brave his wife was through the surgery to remove her brain tumor, and the following Chemo and radiation treatments, until his young daughter could recite them all by heart. But, when he spoke of how her mother died, her daddy always lost it, and something vanished from the translation, as he told how her mother had died. Willow could never quite tell why he was so angry, or how her maternal parent had ended up flying over the Bermuda triangle.

Willow knew nothing of the long search by authorities for the downed plane, which was presumed crashed somewhere. It had disappeared with all aboard...the bodies never found.

She had also been unaware of media harassment of her father, how they tried to sensationalize, accusing him of chasing away his missing wife; they insinuated a disagreement, even made it sound like he was to blame for ALL the deaths. None of it was true, only dramatization; media hype. Willow didn't even realize the lack of privacy in those first years...she was only a mere infant of less than a year.

Nor was she ever aware, of the red tape later to declare her mother dead, so her father could move on with life, and gain the mother's inheritance for his tiny daughter.

For the first four years of her life, Willow lived with the constant preparation for an event, an expedition to clear his name, and find the body that would prove his innocence. Then for two years the idea seemed to drop to the background, until...they actually found the plane...empty.

Now again, she and daddy were heading out. The 'project' was being renewed. They were going out to search the sea bottom for the mother she had never known.

Through the many years, her daddy had trained them both; diving lessons, deep sea excursions, you name it. If it pertained to rescue, Brad took the classes, always bringing along his tiny daughter. Behind the scenes, he instructed her.

At the age of three, Willow was proficient at scuba diving. Even though she was too young to take the classes with him, he taught her afterward, on the side, every bit of knowledge she could absorb. He drilled it into her; a hard task master, never taking into account her age. She must learn it. In later life, he meant for her to be his accomplice. If she couldn't accompany him, he meant to smuggle her in.

As a result, Willow had the education of someone five times her age.

It wasn't that Brad didn't love his daughter; he actually didn't dare let her out of his sight. He feared, if he did, she might go missing , as well. Willow was his last connection to his missing wife...he didn't want to lose that.

Every minute he could spare away from work, every penny saved, even all Willow's inheritance from her mother, had gone to stocking supplies, and preparing for that final object, the last leg of the journey...the 'mission'.

****

Willow was so tired of being expected to be an adult; neglected; more often left alone as not, on a boat, in the hotel room. It was as if she was simply a possession, important only as pertaining to the person of her mother.

She could cook as well as any twenty year old; wash clothes; pack; organize; even schedule trips and book flights. No one at the other end of the internet could tell that she was only seven.

Her home schooling included subjects far beyond that of any university professor, yet all Willow desired was to be permitted to be the child she was.

As they took off into the clouds, she cringed, and the thought went through her head:

Here we go again! Just for once, daddy, I'd like to have a friend my own age. I'd even settle for a new momma, a real home, and brothers and sisters...to play with, as other kids do.

****

Unconsciously, Brad was drumming his fingers impatiently on the arm of the seat, as they took off. In his mind, they couldn't get there fast enough. He wanted to be there diving, and searching. The boat was rented, and waiting at the dock. As they passed over the delightful scenery below, he saw none of it. It didn't register that they were coming into a known resort area, with all the pleasures it entailed. All that was irrelevant! Only Lydia mattered!

The important fact to focus on here, is bringing Lydia home!

It had always felt like she was still living, away somewhere, sending messages back...calling to him. He had nightmares of her fear, and danger, so vivid, he woke, bolting upright, in a cold sweat.

It was no wonder. When they had been together at the end, during her last hospital stays, when she couldn't talk, it was as if he could read her mind; he sensed what she wanted, filled in the words for her when she tried to talk...and he'd always had it right. That was then; why not now?

Lydia would always feel alive to Brad!

Chapter 2

From an early age she had always been told, she had never actually been born. At seven months formed, a Physician aborted her.

Nitha's first vague memories were of probes and forceps; being cut away from inside her mother...the gushing blood; and gasping at air...

They first grew her in a test box until she was large enough to breathe on her own...and suckle...

But, then...she had been rescued...

She remembered her real daddy's great, giant hands ripping her from that glass and metal chamber, removing the tubes, needles, and wires, then soothing her, holding her, naked and shivering, cuddled against his huge chest.

I can still feel that first touch...if I concentrate...

She'd been told, Papa was brown. Momma Jewel has pink skin, and that is why Nitha's is a golden-brown...a combination of them both.

Papa had been simple, and couldn't talk; her real Momma stutters...because of that, Nitha too, rarely speaks.

The Scientists had been experimenting on her; as a result Nitha developed into a telepath.

In Papa's thoughts, she had always been his belly bump. His was the first mind she had ever entered.

Now, her best friend, Thea, talks for her; they communicate mind to mind. That's how Nitha learned to vocalize out loud.

Proudly, Nitha thinks:

We are as sisters; though each is from a different momma.

Thea laughingly cuts in:

Momma Gem calls us girls, Fire and Ice...

All six of us, the four boys, and us two girls, have two mommas between us, but...just one Papa...

Daddy Da died shortly after her birth, as he tried to carry away the boys...

That dreadful Hydra monster got him!

Silence followed. Finally Nitha added:

There is another coming. She will complete the circle...

"Say what? You see that? In the future? Is it a baby?"

Nitha shook her head.

No!

Chapter 3

Little Lee, his legs churning double time, could not stay abreast of the large stepping elder, Scar, for the life of him. The dark skinned older man would not wait, or slow down, even though he knew his companion was having trouble keeping up.

But the six year old half Asian child was used to his treatment.

He wasn't afraid. Even as dark as it was getting, Lee had no fear of the wildlife around them. The soft muted murmurings in the bushes were like another language to him. The animals were calling to their mates, and fellow carnivores, near at hand. They were on the hunt, evening being the time to find a live meal.

Normally, a small boy would be but a mouthful for these large cats, but they both knew and often received, commands from this creature; he was familiar, like a companion beast, and so, they ignored him. They were tracking slower, easier prey, a small Ankylosaurus, plated, yes, but a thick bodied lizard. As it crept through the underbrush, it would be simple for the larger feline predators to catch it, flip it to its back, and gorge themselves on the soft under belly beneath.

Lee disliked when the bigger game took advantage of the weakness of the more helpless. Just for spite, he deviated away from the travelled path, to get nearer to the unaware prey. He warned it, that it was being tracked, mentally sending a thought to the armored baby, and the adolescent lizard slid quietly into a crevasse in the ground, where the cats could not get to him.

It wasn't unusual for Lee to communicate with the animals. That was the unusual talent he possessed. He could also compel any creature to do his bidding, if he chose.

"Don't be so pokey!" growled Scar fearfully. "It's almost dark. Hear those cats? We'll be supper for the wildlife if we don't hurry. Never meant to be out this late! Ah, I see the thorn barrier up ahead...At last!."

"We could have taken to the trees, you know," Lee observed.

Scar grunted, and as they had to go up and over, anyway, he did just that.

The huge, bearded, ape-like Scar was not as tall as Poppa Loni. Scar had a mean temperament, and was a bit slow of mind. He was heavy, muscular, with long arms, and Momma Gem had told Lee, there was a time when Scar only had one arm. Originally, Scar had been one side of conjoined twins.

Galar and he had been separated; as an experiment to see if the two could live apart.

The Overseers did things like that, before all of them died...

The Hydra had eaten Galar...

After the rescue of the children, Loni healed Scar, causing an arm to grow where there had never been one before. Now, Scar could swing through the trees like the Neanderthal he resembled.

At long last, the two dropped into the domestic animal compound.

They had gone out to find a missing set of escaped piglets, who had found a gap in the thorn barrier next to their pen. It didn't take long to realize the tame meat had gone for the wild one's lunch...but the pair had gone a fair ways, and darkness was descending before they reached home.

"Tomorrow," Lee encouraged, to himself. "I get to go to the ocean with Scar."

He much preferred to go fishing. They robbed the still existent traps of the long dead Overseers. In them, was often found unusual surprises: crab and lobster, not indigenous to this planet...however strange and different they were, the crustaceans were mouthwateringly good. Momma Gem knew just how to cook them, so their flesh was not toxic. They had to be boiled alive; they didn't realize they were in hot water until they died, so...they didn't suffer.

Lee had at first felt for them, until he realized, they were unaware of their impending demise.

Chapter 4

"It's starting to rain more heavily," observed Thea aloud. "Storm is real angry with Momma Gem, that she made him stay behind to water the gardens."

Nitha nodded. "More like a hurricane, now; fierce," she thought back. "Wind is picking up... He'll get into trouble again."

That always bothered Thea. Of all the boys, she preferred Storm, with his rebellious character, and the ability to manipulate nature, but she feared he would, someday, go too far. He was not usually a compliant person.

Like Scar, Storm was of darker skin, and resembled the visions she saw, in the minds of her elders, of the dead Overseers of the past.

Peek and Lee were leaving the waters of the lagoon, now, having finished their swim to wash up. They had been extremely dirty from the garden work. All morning, Momma Gem and Jewel had kept them busy weeding the vegetable patches. The six year old boys, of course, did more tunneling in the dirt then anything, so Momma Gem had set them to making the gullies to hold rainwater, between the rows.

Thea heard her Momma in her head, scolding Storm, then calling out to Poppa.

"Loni, where are you? Are you within range?"

It seemed like, they always knew what their foster children were about, even from afar.

"On my way back. I see we have a problem. Storm's out of control, again..."

"We need to find a more ADULT punishment for him..."

Then, the voices went silent, and Thea knew, her parents were cloaking their thoughts, so they could discuss privately.

How can that oversized boy get into so much trouble?

As the other boys joined the girls, in the tree where they were perched, the winds abruptly abated.

Coming up beside Thea, Lee laughed.

"Wonder what punishment he'll get this time?" he mused aloud.

Angered at his attitude, Thea growled back, in defense.

"Now that your outer surface is supposedly clean," she sarcastically shot back. "Maybe, you'd better stay down wind, or...go back to the pig pens, to relieve Scar. No amount of scrubbing will alleviate the smell of barnyard."

Almost immediately, she realized how very cruel the remark was. The Asian look-a-like shrunk his head into his shoulders, turtle-like, in shame.

"Oh, Lee...so sorry." Thea contritely opened her arms to him for a hug.

The older boy obligingly went into them, not refusing the comfort. None of the children ever disagreed for long.

But after only a minute of the sisterly embrace, Lee abruptly drew away, boyishly embarrassed.

"I'd better get back...like you said," he mumbled.

In a flash, he had jumped to the next tree, and was gone.

Chapter 5

The multi-nationals were all finished searching. They had been combing the area almost a year before Brad and Willow had managed to join them, with all the red tape, transfers, and custom officials to placate.

As a qualified diver, Brad managed to slip into the midst of the men and women in the water, just as they were winding down the operation. Leaving his daughter hidden alone on their small pleasure craft, he went below to search the ruins of the plane himself.

Willow remained unnoticed, perhaps mostly because, she never appeared above board until evening, when most of the other divers were back inside, and indulging in well deserved recreation. During each day, she busied herself with cleaning, cooking the meals, and playing video games; ever reading, savoring the alone time, an opportunity to get away from her over dominant father, and his constant appraisal.

When, a week later, the other boats pulled away, no one thought it unusual a lone, small yacht remained behind. The craft appeared deserted; only the last skipper to leave, wondered fleetingly, if those from aboard had possibly abandoned her. But, it being none of his business, he went on his way, resolving to return in a week or so. If it was still there, it would then, become his salvage.

Toward evening, Brad surfaced, and while partaking of the meal prepared by his daughter, he shared the thought, he planned to go down one more time, to check out a huge sand hill, some distance beyond the wreck site on the ocean floor.

Next morning, he vanished again beneath the waves...once more abandoning his seven year old to her own devices.

Chapter 6

Water gurgled, shifted like waves around him. The seaweed obstructed his view. Brad pushed it aside.

This isn't a sand hill at all!

He moved into the opening cautiously, shining his head piece so the lamp lit both above, and then his path, This first section seemed made of an accordion-coil, covered by some sort of rubberized water-proof plastic. It led into a larger dome-like structure, with broken down balconies rising in tiers, above him. It resembled the city malls back home, or an airport terminal.

What the heck is this doing here?

For a good twenty minutes, Brad swam along the weedy pathway, leading through the place. Then, he came upon a doorway, the door hanging askew. He noticed a lighted mirror-like archway, just inside, on the wall opposite the doorway. Curiosity had him passing into the small closet, before he had reasoned, whether it was safe. Next thing, he was drawn through the brilliant arch, as if compelled...to the other side.

Brad had the oddest sensation...of traveling through time, and space...stars all about, speeding past fast; blackness beyond that; planets...and then, he was someplace else, water no longer about him, only cloudy air, with feather tendrils of smoke, everywhere.

He stood up to walk, but left his breathing apparatus on.

Above him, once again, were the many tiers of balconies, where at a bygone time, there might have been passengers waiting. He pictured men and women gazing down at him, as he traversed the long winding path through, but almost all of the platforms above were decrepit, rails broken, foundations cracked or with gaping holes. The whole place appeared to have undergone a tremendous cataclysmic event.

And then, shocked, Brad abruptly stopped short.

Oh, friggen h! Did I just see a decaying body up there?

Hanging suspended, the boney hand still attached to a broken rail, far above...yes! That WAS a body!

Brad cursed, and began to move on again.

What the hell happened here?

Then a thought hit him.

This might be where the bodies from the plane are!

But...it was near impossible to get up there, and...he could tell, even from here, the bones were not that of a female: feet too large; waist too wide; thick chest...no, not a woman. And Brad was looking specifically for Lydia.

****

Willow waited a week, impatient and lonely...but, she wasn't afraid. However, the thought did go through her mind:

Maybe, my dad isn't coming back.

Brad had trained her for such an emergency; schooled her in the sailing of the small pleasure craft. If he ever failed to appear, she was to head to the nearest marina, and take the chance of alerting authorities.

But...before she went to that extreme, Willow felt she owed it to her father, to go below, to be reassured, that the ocean hadn't actually robbed her of that second parent.

Maybe, somehow, my father found the hole mom dropped through, and he is now as lost as the mother I never knew.

Despite being merely seven, Willow was as well trained in underwater submersion as any adult. She had accompanied Brad on every course or undersea exercise he had taken; her father had reviewed all he learned by taking his young daughter out on a similar dive afterward, drilling into her, in minute detail, the same instructions he had received.

Willow had her own equipment, a smaller version of her dad's gear: flippers, wetsuit, goggles, oxygen tanks, even headlamp and underwater weapons. After careful preparation, the petite young girl followed her missing parent into the ocean.

She knew all the risks, how, when returning, she would have to rise to the surface slowly, so as to keep away the 'bends'; the reaction of the body to too rapid a pressure change. From infancy, she'd been raised on deep-sea diving; fear was never a factor; it was rejected and frowned upon by her father.

Giant sea creatures were like playthings to her; they had been her companions since early childhood. They were non threatening. Willow mostly ignored them, swimming in among them without trepidation.

The darkness was chased away by her headlamp; cold was something she steeled against; but, her body simply adapted. After all she was young.

Down went Willow; down; down, not even stopping at the wreckage.

She knew, he wouldn't be there!

She was aware her mother had perished here, but she wasn't even curious.

Her mission was to find the living...or a MALE body!

Coldly, she analyzed the situation.

Through the murky, frigid waters, she passed, direct to the hump of sand. It was fully as tall as a man, even more. In fact, now she was nearby, the mound looked at least twenty feet tall.

Floating in place, treading water, Willow looked about.

She fully expected to find a floating, bloated creature, eyes staring vacantly, caught under or by a piece of abandoned wreckage. Callously, she reasoned:

What difference would it make to lose this parent? All my life, he has never seen me. I am a means to an end; not a person...I am forever alone, anyway...

Instead of a dead father, Willow found a buried cable. She followed it around the side of the hill. On the other side, near invisible here under water, Brad had marked the entrance with a small suspended buoy.

A large bush of seaweed nearly obscured the opening where the cable went into the obsidian darkness beneath.

Chapter 7

Willow, forewarned by countless like situations during her training, decided not to follow her father into the obvious trap.

What if he's not even in there, and I get stuck instead? There is no one to help me! He may have only marked this entrance to explore later, and cased the outside first. That's what he usually does.

Taking that route, she proceeded along the extended side of the sand barrier, where she came upon a second opening. Unmarked, this one was much smaller.

Perhaps, dad has already explored the first entrance...he's probably in here.

Wisely, she thought, the young girl first tethered herself to a firm handle, attached to a piece of buried debris, nearby, then wound the rope about her waist. Only then, did she cautiously enter.

She did not hear the click, as the lever moved back into a slot.

Willow found nothing inside, but the dark interior of a closet-like box. As she went to turn around and return the way she had come, there was a blinding flash of light.

Suddenly, the tether keeping her safe was severed, and Willow was inside a new open space; a large warehouse, and...the water had vanished.

This time, the click of the switch was clearly audible; the grinding of gears, then from above her, before Willow could even duck, dropped a huge net, scooping her up, suspending her in mid air. She was slowly moved along, like some weird fish, and transported, to be dumped, as the net slackened and opened, into a pile of salt, sand, and...crustaceans.

The air in the room was frigid cold. Willow still wore her wet suit, flippers, and other gear, but even so, she felt the change in temperature on her bare cheeks.

She tried to crawl from the encasing grey grains encompassing her, but they held like quicksand, and the more she struggled the deeper she sank.

Prudently, the girl stopped moving, judging it best for her own safety.

It appeared she was in some sort of fisherman's trap; he must check it daily.

Surely, someone will come soon, and free me.

After a time, even through the wetsuit, Willow felt the deep cold. Soon, she was shivering. Her face mask began to fog up, restricting her vision.

When the oxygen gave out, Willow finally removed the mask and her air tanks, let them drop into the salt beside her. They slipped into the colorless sand, and abruptly, a hole opened around her, and she began slide down with it. By reflex, the girl drew in a quick breath, ceased to struggle, going deathly still. She knew if she didn't, she would go under.

Hours later, all but the child's head was deep in the salt pile. She was numbed to the bone, both from staying so rigid, and the paralyzing cold. Mercifully, sleep, also, had slipped in to help time pass.

****

Lee was excited, as he rapidly passed through the dark tunnels of the underground fishery. Scar had allowed him to check the far ice cooler on his own. It was rare the man treated him like an adult, but they had had a large catch today, and the older man was over weary, and...too lazy to go all that way.

As Lee entered, the great, rusty, steel door squealed complainingly. Catching up a wicker basket, twice his size, the six year old went to the shifting switch on the wall, that operated the winch mechanism. Lee flipped it, and the metal claw came down over the eight foot tall salt pile. He dropped it carefully, one side of the open claw beside each wall. The boy knew, if it came together violently, the crustaceans imprisoned there would come out nothing but mush.

As the huge grabber began to come together, Lee suddenly spied the small human head sticking from the white sand. At first he refused to believe his eyes.

What is Nitha doing here? Is this a trick? Dumb girls!

Before the claw could do her harm, Lee shut the mechanism off.

****

Willow opened her eyes at the sound of the gears taking hold. In the corner, by the door, stood a boy about a year younger than she.

He was Asian, not very big for his age, with yellowish skin, slanted eyes, and straight black hair, cut short. All he wore, were shorts of some sort of animal skin; his chest and feet bare, and a band around his forehead, containing a light lamp, causing his figure to be illuminated, so she could clearly see him. His mouth hung open stupidly, as if in shock.

He yelled something unintelligible; she didn't understand, but called out to him in her own tongue, anyway.

"Help me! I don't dare move. It sucks me under..."

The boy grunted with annoyance; then answered in the language she had used.

"Funny. You think this some sort of joke? Why use verbal...and in this old tongue? Where are the other girls?"

"I'm the only one here," she shouted back, puzzled. "No others came with me..."

"Kinda of stupid to come in here alone," he scolded. "Can't you jump out? I thought Thea taught you that..."

"No!" Willow returned, annoyed now by his stupidity. "This salt is too tight around me."

"Never stops Thea..." After a frown, and a moment of thought, he went on slowly. "Say... You hit your head or something? You sure seem addled..."

Gosh! What an insulting boy!

"I heard that! You know what Momma says about belittling others. I've had enough of it; first Thea, and then you. I've half a mind to leave you here..."

He wouldn't really leave me here, would he?

"Just mad enough to..."

For a second, Willow puzzled over his remarks, but realization topped even her danger.

"You can read thoughts?"

"Course I can! I'm as telepathic as you. Just because I work with Scar doesn't make me an imbecile."

Another silence followed, in which the boy appeared to be reasoning out something. When he spoke again, he was still analyzing, only out loud.

"How come...you aren't stuttering? You're not Nitha, are you? She stutters, like her Momma, when she goes verbal...Who are you? Where did you come from?"

"I have no idea who Nitha is...and, I've never had a speech impediment in my life. So, for your information...I came from the marina. I arrived in a boat; simpleton! I'm looking for my father! I got caught by your stupid trap! Now, tell me where he is! Get me out of here; and take me to him!"

He walked closer, the better to see her; staying silent; observing her.

"No; you're definitively not the Nitha I know;" he observed , quietly. "She's far more gentle... Unless this is some sort of act... If Momma Gem hadn't taught us not to mind invade, I'd have entered your memories already. I'll put a stop to your lies! This world is empty, except for us! No intelligent other beings...only the bodies of Overseers!"

Willow was shook to the core.

Where am I? That flash of light...did it take me...somewhere else?

"You went through a portal?"

"Yes," she answered hesitantly. "I think so..."

He grunted, and frowned, then half under his breath, muttered: "Thought the portals weren't working no more..."

He turned about, walked to the mechanism, turning it back on.

"Stay still. I'll bring the claw down over you...by the way, I'm Lee..."

"Willow."

Lee nodded. Slowly, inch by inch, he maneuvered the claw until it was directly above her, then delicately encased her head.

"Don't move...don't want to break your neck..."

Terrified, Willow wanted desperately to squirm, to scream, but she decided not to let fear get the better of her. She too, had been trained...well!

When he had deposited her at his feet, Lee shut down the machine.

****

He shook his head in wonderment.

Man! Does she ever look like Nitha! I think she's older, though.

"Are you older than me?" Lee demanded.

"Depends how old you are..."

"Six."

"I'm seven and a half."

"So you're about two years older than Nitha..."

"Who is this Nitha you keep talking about?" Willow fired back in annoyance. "Why do you keep using her as your guide, as if she's the only girl you know."

"You look like her...she's one of my foster sisters..."

"Okay..."

She didn't voice the questions, Lee knew must be there on the tip of her tongue, so he decided to claim leadership of this partnership right from the first.

"If you expect to stay alive, here in my world, you'll need to do what I say. You hear?"

"And if I don't?"

"I'll sigg the animals on you!"

The boy was aware, if Momma Gem heard what he was saying, he'd catch it for his dominating approach; it was both unfair to Willow, and extremely rude, but Lee felt it was needed. If Scar came on the scene, this girl would soon learn, the hard way, not to cross him.

With me as boss over her, she will be much safer...if she obeys.

"First thing," Lee decided. "You need to take off that rubber suit. Scar won't like that; he'll think you're an Overseer come back to life. He detests the Overseers."

****

Willow wasn't about to contradict him. There was no telling just what kind of animal he had in his control, nor what he, himself, could do to her. She wasn't taking any chances.

This Scar might be a big cat for all I know...I don't want to be eaten.

Obediently, Willow quickly unzipped, peeling down to the naked, letting her skintight suit drop to the floor around her ankles.

It isn't as if a seven year old is a woman yet, even though my nipples are beginning to bud.

Lee's jaw went slack at the sudden exposure, and he quickly turned away in embarrassment.

"What? You never see a girl strip before?"

He gulped, still keeping his eyes turned away.

"Didn't know you had nothing on underneath. We give our sisters privacy..."

"Well, it's kind of hard to wear something beneath this..."

"Man!" Lee exclaimed, suddenly coming alive. "We got to get you something to wear...before...before, Scar sees you..." He was still mumbling as he made for the door. "Stay here! I think there are coveralls in the next room..."

When Lee left, wearing the headlamp, Willow became acutely aware of the frigid warehouse, like a freezer turned as low as possible. The room also went black as pitch. She stood there shivering, unable to see anything.

He was back directly, still boyishly embarrassed, holding out a pair of rough coveralls, his eyes averted. The garment proved two sizes too big, but Willow improvised, folding the leggings up to the right length. At least it was a comfortable covering.

****

Scar had dozed off while waiting for Lee. He snorted awake, when the boy touched his shoulder, near jumping from his skin with the sudden fright.

The boy wasn't alone; he had Nitha with him.

"What's she doing here?" Scar growled grumpily. "You know, I'm not supposed to go near the girls."

"She's not Nitha; her name's Willow."

"Like heck! You two think you can play any trick on me! Well, fine! I'll play along. I punish for jokes, you know, little princess," he snarled in her face, for effect. "You'll work alongside Lee, and as hard...just as if they appointed you to me! Take the other end of the tub; both of you! Didn't get any fish?" he asked of Lee.

"Nothing there..."

The female hid behind Lee, as though she hadn't understood. Scar made a feint, as if to strike her. Lee stepped between them protectively, and directed her to the handles on the opposite side of the metal basket.

Scar turned his back, so he wouldn't see them, and started out of the warehouse.

Stupid kids, anyway!

Chapter 8

Brad had come into a maze of underground caves, which he followed for hours. Fearing to get lost, he finally began dropping pieces of his gear behind him, to mark the way back; never anything he needed, simply a clamp, or a link of chain, he could do without.

Finally, when the air around him, seemed to have cleared somewhat, Brad dared to remove his face mask and breather. He found he could safely breathe the air, though he smelled the odor of burnt wire and chemicals. He left the apparatus suspended around his neck.

At that point, he noted ladders fastened against the cement walls, rising up at intervals. At the moment, he was passing through damaged, empty, gigantic vats. Brad suspected, they were the source of the chemical smell, so he chose to take one of these risers upward, for his own safety.

He climbed easily, even though some of the rungs were broken or missing, and located a second floor above the first. He was amazed by what he found on that level; a monstrous garden stretched off in the distance, for what seemed like miles.

Far above he glimpsed sunlight. Though dim and anemic, the light appeared to be coming through dome-like, iron rafters, covered with broken Plexiglas, all of which was overgrown by a vine-like growth.

The thought went through his head, that he might have stumbled into an abandoned greenhouse, but...

Man! This is no ordinary grow-op! The support system beneath this, alone, would need to be incredibly sturdy.

The trees in this section were mostly mature fruit trees; had to have been there for years. At some time, they were laden down with produce, but they had been forsaken, and with no one to tend them, the fruit, after rotting, had dropped, and along with the fallen leaves, had created a mush of decay. This had dried, entrapping odors and rancid liquid beneath. It rose up as you passed across, squishing out over your footwear; the fumes assaulting your nose.

Some place farther on, Brad found another ladder going up. His flippers were annoying him, all cover in putrid goo. They made it difficult to walk, so at the foot of this riser, he abandoned them, left them, both to mark his back-path, and to make it easier to go up another level. He continued in bare feet.

He came out over a huge waterfall, and here, he found evidence of an old deserted campsite. At the side of the falls was a sectioned off, small pool, obviously meant to catch fresh drinking water.

In the middle of the place was a campfire, with a small tee-pee of metal set up over dry kindling, waiting to be lit. Beside this a pair of boots sat, as if drying by the fire, just waiting for him. It appeared as if those staying here had left in a hurry.

Brad sat down to try on the boots. They fit, so he kept them on.

Neglected, under two enormous spruce trees, were decaying mats, obviously for sleeping, and across these, tin cups, plates, and various toiletries, had been strewn, as if abandoned quickly.

What made them leave in such a hurry? What were they running from?

There was even a chocolate bar dropped among the mess. It made Brad realized how hungry he was. He sat down again, pulled a string of beef jerky from his belt pack at his waist, and began to chew away at it.

He sat there pondering.

Should I go on, or...go back?

He was decidedly curious; wanted the answer to the riddle.

This is evidence of a complicated civilization, all under water. Perhaps, this is Atlantis? Intelligent people used to dwell here...maybe, some still remain...and possibly...this is where the survivors from the plane ended up? Lydia might be among them...

That settled it! He was going on!

Brad stood to his feet, and spying another rusted ladder, over at the side, rising up, he went to it, and started climbing.

****

He did not expect the horror he encountered. In the next few minutes, Brad crossed through what appeared to be an old nursery. It had obviously been abandoned hurriedly, and the tiny infants left behind: tiny cadavers in cribs, curled in the fetal position, as if each had died in its sleep.

Horrified, he moved horizontally, hoping to rapidly vacate the area. Next, he entered an operating room, where he found a still clothed skeleton of a physician on his feet, bent over the bones of a woman laying flat on a table, knees up and wide spread. Between her legs was a minute infant, arms raised, as if squalling. All were frozen in time, at the exact moment of birth, of a baby that had never gotten to experience life.

Brad shivered with revulsion, hurrying on.

What happened here? What caused this traumatic sudden ending?

Brad finally found a ladder leading down again. Litterly fleeing, he descended to another passage. It was not the one he had left earlier.

****

For hours, he had been lost, when suddenly Brad opened a door, and found an immense slaughter house.

What is this place? That they even had cattle...

But the bones on the cutting table were not those of cows or pigs.

Is that what I think it is? That can't be a human foot? No way!

This section was no better than the nurseries.

Was this like a breeding farm...for humans? Oh, gosh! I got to get out of here! There has to be a way out.

Brad had to admit, there was no way he wanted to retrace his steps; he'd have to find another way.

****

At long last, he had found a way that led up again. He could see light above.

Brad had come to a ledge, traversed along it, where he had found a discarded, small, empty, dilapidated wagon at the foot of a ladder going up. It gave him hope.

This must be the way out!

He climbed the ladder, emerging from the top, on to a second ledge, only to find...it was a dead end.

Chapter 9

As Brad surveyed his new surroundings, he had the uncomfortable feeling he was being watched, yet he could see no one in the tree across the way. However, the reality of finding where he actually was, drove that awareness to the back of his mind.

No way, am I still on the planet Earth! How the hell did that happen?

Stretched before him, far into the distance, were the strangest trees. They appeared to be standing up-side-down, the roots in the air, reaching for the heavens, even though these were covered in leaves. And the color of the foliage was all wrong; coppers, oranges, and shades of fuchsia, the trunks a dark purple, as if here...it was perpetually fall. But the sky was the oddest. It had a purple-blue hue, as if everything was under a late evening fog.

Yet, it was actually early morning. He could see a huge tangerine sun rising above the horizon.

Once again, Brad had the uncomfortable feeling of being watched. He scanned the trees.

Under the leaves, it was as black as pitch.

Then, under the branches of a tree across the ravine, he saw the shifting of shadow. Uncertain of what he had seen, Brad studied the next tree. No movement.

There is no wind!

He jerked his eyes back to the first tree, and the area of movement...and caught just the slightest shift.

Oh, this guy is good!

"Hey you! Show yourself!"

Two brown-black orbs blinked open, revealing the whites of eyes, but nothing else. Brad couldn't make out the face, but...he had been right!

Yet, by the size of the eyes, the sentry was either a tree monkey, or...a midget human being.

Unless...it is a child?

Being used to having control, Brad forcefully commanded:

"Show yourself!"

And suddenly, as if the curt order had been too frightful, the eyes vanished.

Sadly, Brad sat down to wait; there was no place else to go.

He had scared away the only prospect for interaction.

****

The man sat there, for what seemed like hours, waiting for the creature to return. He figured the curiosity would prove irresistible. It was best to stay, anyway, rather than get lost in the caverns again, as there was no way across to the other side.

Brad could see the remnants of a broken bridge, hanging from a tree on the opposite side, but no other way forward. He reasoned, this was evidence, there was civilized life of some sort here, or at least, there had been.

So he continued to wait.

It was near evening; already growing dark, when something finally happened.

The sky was now even stranger; stars in rings around the planet; two moons , one moving slower across the sky than the other.

Suddenly, the tiny eyes were back. Brad grinned. His wait had been successful!

But then, a second pair of eyes appeared beside the first. These were turquoise, and the whites glowed out of the darkness, an almost pale mauve hue.

"Hey! You!" Brad demanded. "Can you understand me? Talk to me!"

It felt like a wave of sound exploding in his head; a powerful voice directed right into his mind.

"Who are you? Where did you come from?"

Brad answered in the only way he knew how; out loud, and in his own language.

"I came through the tunnels...I think I'm no longer on my world. But...I mean you no harm," he added quickly. "I don't know how to get back out...fact is, I'm not certain how I even got here."

Silence was his only answer. For some time, the one behind the voice pondered on the situation. At last, it spoke again.

"Are there more than one of you?"

"No. Just me."

****

Loni found the man's controlling attitude offensive, right from the first. He was too sure of himself; too bossy. Loni noted this in his body language, without reading deeply into his mind. It was, 'obey me or else!' and Loni didn't like such men; they reminded him of the Overseers. The man's lack of consideration for the opinion of others made him a danger to himself, and those around him.

His appearance resembled an Overseer, as well, with his darkly tanned skin, and hazel eyes, but his build was different, shoulders not so stooped, as the guards of the past; stood with his feet apart, challengingly, just as they always had. But, this human was far more fit; tall and solid, with well developed chest and arms, abdomen flat.

If Loni needed to control him, and he was uncooperative, Loni would physically find it difficult.

Yet, the leader of the Azure Blue encampment realized he could not simply leave this man out here, shouting to the wind. He would surely awaken the Hydra, and then all would pay. Against his better judgment, Loni moved forward, and dropped the new bridge they had just finished constructing.

It had been rolled in the notch of the tree behind. Using his levitation beam beneath the slats, Loni guided the hooked end, from their tree to the cliff shelf.

The human was totally unaware that this conveyance had been guided over by mind control. He was watching its top, as it moved over the expanse, and missed, entirely, the source of the blue beam beneath.

Both Peek and Loni held their breath, as the human clamored noisily across, his heavy boots scraping, and pounding clumsily against the branch-like flooring.

Loni recognized the footwear. The boots had once belonged to Scar, abandoned for the exact same reason that was obvious at the moment. Apparently, at some point, the man had commandeered the hunting boots from their old campsite, inside.

Finally, the human was across.

Thank goodness! The Hydra must be asleep, or hunting elsewhere. If it was below, this man would not have lived this long.

For a moment, the man startled, unprepared, as tiny, black skinned Peek came out of hiding from the tree behind. With the rope, that was attached to the ledge hooks, Peek pulled back the make-shift draw bridge, rolled it up, and stowed it, once again, in the crotch of the tree.

"Hey," the newcomer commandingly suggested. "Just leave it up, so we can come and go more easily?"

Annoyed at his assuming control, Loni simply stared at him, not wanting a confrontation. It seemed the man thought he was the better equipped to lead.

"Be quiet!" Loni finally hissed aloud. "You have no sense of danger...Do you intend to wake all the sleeping prowlers?"

"There are predators here? Where?" the man quickly returned, belligerently. "Seems pretty quiet to me..."

Loni turned to his small black companion.

"Let him hear what you do, Peek!"

The six year old grinned. He realized, this would be of great amusement, and Peek loved a prank.

"Listen, human!" Loni ordered in the other man's head.

After a moment, the man said aloud.

"I don't hear nothing..."

Man! He's deaf, as well, as stupid!

Loni amplified the sound: beneath the tree where they sat, a snarling cat coughed; then far in the distance, the howl of wolves could be heard, encouraging each other to bravery, and lastly, the trumpet call of a huge Tyrannosaurus Rex, calling to its mate, as they hunted smaller prey.

The new member's eyes grew wider, with each additional sound, then showed astonishment, and finally, outright alarm.

"What was that last call? Never heard anything like it; don't recognize it."

"T-Rex," Peek volunteered, his face a picture of seriousness, though he had all he could do not to burst into laughter. He had gotten the reaction he hoped for.

"Oh, come on!" laughed the newcomer. "No such thing living still."

Loni shook his head, disgusted.

What will it take to convince this man? What am I suppose to do with the idiot?

Loni turned to Peek.

"Go home, little Warrior. You need not watch tonight," Loni spoke gently, comfortingly, direct to the boy's mind, but allowed the man also to hear. "Tell Momma Gem, I will remain out this night..."

"'K."

****

As the miniature black boy quickly vanished into the dark foliage, Brad took a second look at the man beside him. Against the night sky, he was like a ghost, his skin a pale bluish white. He had irises the color of turquoise, the pupil going vertical, like those of a cat, and the white around the eye was a mauve-white hue that glowed in the dark. His face was heart shaped, beardless; his head topped by curly white-blond hair. His oddest feature was; he had no ears.

He appeared but a boy, but somehow, Brad realized, he was much older; how old, the Earthman couldn't determine. The creature was humanoid, skinny, yet athletic in appearance, and as tall as Brad. That meant he was over six feet. He wore shorts, of some unrecognizable animal skin, and carried no weapons.

"I am Loni," he revealed in mind talk. "What are you called?"

"Brad."

The human extended his hand, but rather than taking it, Loni turned away, looking out over the tree tops, after the boy.

"You just let him go alone?" quizzed Brad, dropping his hand.

If he wants to be unfriendly, fine.

"Aren't you afraid the boy will be eaten? Or, did you just make up those sounds to shut me up?"

Loni turned to him.

"I watch him with my mind...until he's safe."

"Okay..."

"And the sounds were real; animals genuine...they are dangerous!"

"Fine! I believe you. Now, what?"

"Come with me, and...try not to be so noisy. I do not wish to be supper for the cats."

Brad chuckled, envisioning in his head, the blue skinned, skinny male on a large platter, felines sitting about the table with fork and knife.

He wouldn't be more than a mouthful.

Loni hissed, as if he'd seen the image...or read his thought.

Can he read me?

Loni turned away, started across a metal and slat bridge, that had been hidden behind the tree. Brad was forced to hurry to keep up to him.

After going over two such walkways, past a dome-like hut in a tree, suddenly, Loni stopped short abruptly. Brad nearly ran into him.

The man turned about in annoyance, and pointing at Brad's feet; the loud words nearly shouted to his mind.

"Take them off! Please." The tone softened, then. "They are too loud. The cat below still follows."

Brad realized Loni was quite serious, so he sat on the swaying bridge, and removed his boots.

"Give," Loni demanded, holding out his hand.

Brad was surprised that he wanted to carry his shoes. He was even more shocked, when Loni tossed them over his shoulder into the darkness.

"Hey! I might need those!"

Loni growled at Brad, snarling like he was a wild dog, and Brad quickly got to his feet, backing up in uncertainty.

It was the first verbal sound of aggression Brad had heard from Loni, and it made the hair on the back of his neck rise up in foreboding.

What have I gotten myself into here? I'm alone with this guy.

Mind you, I'm heavier than he is, and...I have a gun.

The voice in his head came low and ominous this time.

"You don't want to mess with me, human! I just may have weapons you cannot see..."

Brad's jaw dropped; his eyes widened. He said no more.

Loni turned about, and rapidly moved away, as if he'd just had enough. If it had not been for his blue-white skin, Brad would have quickly lost him in the darkness.

They finally reached another dome-shaped building in a tree. Loni stepped aside so Brad could enter. Inside, it was empty except for a few rough mats, and furs, piled in a corner on the floor.

"Sleep, now," Loni commanded.

For the first time in days, Brad stopped to evaluate, and realized the extent of his fatigue. He hadn't slept since he'd gone down beneath the ocean near the underwater wreck. Brad was quite willing to rest; dropped down to the nearest mat, and sat there, waiting for the other man to join him.

But, apparently, Loni had other plans.

Brad finally lay down in impatience, closing his eyes.

Loni was still sitting at the entrance, gazing out at the distant sky, when Brad awoke the next morning, to the brilliant light of a tangerine sun.

Chapter 10

Lydia rose up from a crouch beside the brazier, where she was frying meat. As he entered the cook shack with Loni, she startled when she saw the second man. Emitting a soft squeak of shocked surprise, she backed away in sudden alarm, recognizing Brad.

But, he appeared not to know her. He followed Loni into the shadowed interior.

"No need to fear, Jewel," Loni reassured to her mind, and she knew, he was also allowing Brad to hear the words.

Loni had called her by this favorite name since the babies had been able to understand. It was easier for their little minds to configure this moniker.

"We found this man," Loni continued. "By the Hydra cliff, alone. I could not leave him. Better he is with us, then he become our enemy."

He turned to Brad. "If you work, we will feed you...and you can sleep among us."

"Okay." Brad answered out loud. "Just show me what you want done."

"First, eat!"

As the two men dropped to the floor cross-legged, to receive their portions, the children soundlessly trouped in; the boys first; the girls following: Peek and Storm; Thea and Nitha, E-ri behind. Lee, who was appointed to help Scar, had been fed much earlier.

At sight of Nitha, Brad shot to his feet with an expletive on his lips.

"How the HELL did YOU get here?" he exclaimed in shock. "And..." He frowned. "Ahead of me, yet?"

The five year old girl backed away, frightened, quickly hiding behind her eight year old foster brother, E-ri.

Ignoring E-ri, Brad went behind him, grabbing Nitha by the arm, forcefully.

"I told you to stay on the boat! You know better than to disobey in a situation like this."

The air was like a thunderstorm brewing, with lightning about to strike. Suddenly, those of blue-white complexion were in challenge mode, rigid, as if about to unleash hidden weaponry: Loni; E-ri, and even, five year old, Thea. Six year old, Storm, the brown-skinned fellow, and little Peek were close behind them, in a posture of defense, all circling, and crowding in on the disputing pair.

The children would allow Loni to move in first. That was always their usual method. E-ri would move in second, if Loni failed.

But Brad was totally unconscious of his danger. Suddenly, he looked up, startled, and realized his precarious position...attempted to explain.

"She's my daughter..."

Loni shook his head in vehement disagreement.

"Not your daughter! That is Nitha!"

He hissed aloud; though he had spoken non-verbally.

"Stand down!"

Unconvinced, Brad demanded of Nitha.

"Tell them!"

Tears formed in the young child's eyes; Nitha tried to back away, but Brad held tenaciously to her forearm.

"Stand down!" growled Loni, his voice like thunder in Brad's brain.

"Tell them," pleaded Brad, insistently. "What is the matter with you, anyway?"

"I...not," stuttered Nitha.

Shocked, Brad abruptly released her, backing away. He raised his hands, palms outward, in a form of defense, and submission, meant to appease Loni.

"Okay...okay. I'm sorry. She looks the spitting image of my daughter, Willow..."

Lydia's heart leap to her throat.

MY Willow? My Willow is here? And you left her above...alone on a boat?

She then, as Gem had trained her, quickly veiled her thoughts. Loni was too busy concentrating on the intrusive events, to pick up on her mind wanderings, of the moment.

At that moment, Gem entered the lunch room dome. The conversation that followed was carried out in silence, and between Loni and Gem, an explanation of what had gone before. Perhaps, E-ri and Thea were privy to some of it, but they too, kept it to themselves. It was not unusual for the blue skinned telepaths to converse so; it was easier for them to communicate more rapidly, apart.

As Loni spiritedly brought Gem up to speed, and she mollified him by her gentle approach to the danger, the children visibly relaxed.

Finally, Loni was reassured by Gem's apparent unconcern, and moved again to Brad's side. Dismissing whatever was worrying the male, the female turned, quickly making a suggestion aloud.

"Shall we eat?"

****

With the meal over, the structure now reverted from a cafeteria to a family room. The children gathered around a small puzzle game, and soundlessly began to play, while the one boy, Storm, seemed relegated to helping Gem wash the dishes. His submissive attitude toward this appointment, amazed Brad, and so did the group's attention to cleanliness.

Most surprising was the fact, Loni curled up in a far corner, and was soon fast asleep. The room was unbelievably silent, the family muting their behavior to meet the elder's need.

However, as Brad watched them, he realized they were still, somehow, silently conversing.

Telepaths? Like the man, Loni?

The small black child, Peek, sat down beside him.

"You are part right," he agreed in a whisper. "Those of blue skin are telepaths, but the rest of us have also been taught the practice. It is more safe to be silent when outside, so we converse non-verbal."

"I guess you can all read minds, too, apparently. Doesn't it bother you, that you are invading the privacy of another?"

"We read limitedly, but you are unguarded. We have been taught not to intrude... You still need to be shown how to cloak, project, and to read."

"Sorry, buddy, but most humans don't learn such things..."

"Gem and Jewel came from human, and we are all of experiments in human DNA. Loni will teach you, too..." As Brad looked toward the sleeping man, Peek added: "when he wakes up."

Brad grunted, doubtful. After a space of silence, he finally asked the question on his mind.

"Most of you look about the same age; yet you are all clearly of different parents...how did that come about? And...just what happened out there?"

"When we were babies, we were in the nurseries, all together. The scientists were experimenting, trying to enhance our abilities to make it possible for all to be more productive. But, shortly after we were born, the domes were sabotaged; a series of explosions destroyed them. It was a great disaster..."

Brad nodded.

"I saw evidence of that, as I came through."

"Loni, Gem and Jewel...and one other, did their best to save as many babies as they could. Da, Nitha's father died...he was very brave..."

"Were these guys, the Scientists?"

"Oh, never! No! Those of the blue skin race were slaves, outcasts... The dark ones...they look like

Storm...were the Overseers, and...they were not telepaths. They despised telepaths; tried...always, killed them...if a person showed signs of mental advancement, they were executed."

Brad frowned.

A war between telepaths and...normal?

"So, where are the rest of these adults?" he wondered aloud. "Those responsible for saving you?"

"This is all that are left."

"Two women, and one man?" Brad demanded, incredulous. "Brought all these children out? And took care of them?"

Peek nodded.

"We were babies...each carried two or three..."

"Holy cow!" Brad exclaimed, astonished, then quickly lowered his voice. "How the Hell did they manage it?"

"Those of blue skin have powers we do not possess..."

Okay. Something to file away for future concern...

"So...both women...belong to Loni?"

The small black boy frowned.

Oh, of course. He's too young to know what I mean.

Unnoticed by Brad, E-ri, the older blue skinned boy, had crept up behind him. As the child spoke, Brad gave a start.

"Loni and Gem are our only pair! It is forbidden to be intimate with a female!"

So the older boy is aware.

E-ri glared at him.

"And You will neither insult, nor assault, our women, whether young or old!"

Brad actually felt intimidated. He knew better than to ask what would happen.

"So...how OLD are you?" Brad meant to sidetrack, but the boy would have none of it.

"I am eight. My name is E-ri," the older boy stated tersely. "It means 'protector'."

It didn't surprise Brad that the boy took his name seriously.

"And Peek, is six."

"So...this all took place about five or six years ago?"

"Yes."

"And...how old are the others?"

"Storm and Lee are six, as well. The girls are five."

"Lee; so there is another boy? Where is he?"

"With Scar. They tend the livestock."

"So, there is another man?" Brad assumed.

""Scar is no man! He is an it. Neither male or female. He was half of a pair of joined twins. The Physicians experimented to see if they could live separate, and cut them apart. The Hydra eat the other...the male half."

Brad shivered at the implication behind the words.

"So...Scar is female?"

"No!" declared E-ri disgustedly, as if the very thought Brad suggested was abhorrent. "Of course not! They gave him no privates."

Puzzled, Brad sat there, trying to envision the man described. At last, he gave up. The other revelation from E-ri finally returned to his mind.

"You said, 'Hydra', didn't you? That's a mythical creature said to guard Hades."

The older boy grinned.

"Very real, here. I have faced it," E-ri boasted.

"No way!"

Suddenly, as if the thought had reawakened a memory dream, across the room, Loni began thrashing out in his sleep. He abruptly sat up, looking about him in a confused manner. Immediately, Gem dried her hands, and quickly moved to his side. Soothing him gently, she lay down, in front of him, her back to him. In a most natural action, Loni reached out, gathering her in his arms. Before long, each closed their eyes, falling asleep, spoon-like together.

Taking control, with his foster parents out of the picture, E-ri rose to his feet.

"We must go, now," he declared emphatically.

"Where?" Brad asked, somewhat annoyed.

"To the gardens...to weed," E-ri challenged.

Brad shrugged, and obediently got to his feet to follow.

The woman, Jewel, also joined them at the door. As if E-ri in command was not unusual, shooing the girls out ahead of them, she spoke not a word to Brad.

Chapter 11

Scar's main purpose in life was self-preservation, the desire to survive whatever it took. He knew he was disliked by the blue skinned leaders, and that wore like an open sore in his mind. He felt, Gem and Loni still held it against him, for kidnapping little Nitha when she was first born. They would never let him alone with the young females; always his helpers were the boys.

Secondly, he felt they did not trust him, because in a temper tantrum of revenge, when Loni had angrily sent him packing, Scar had set the charges that had began the earthquakes, destroying their world below. Loni blamed Scar that those first years, food had been so scarce. He often said, while they learned to hunt, and set up the safe barriers, if the children had not been babies, none would have survived.

For a long time, Scar had held a grudge, just waiting for the chance to retaliate. He obeyed, but kept to himself. And now, finally, he had one up on his leader. He had this girl; he could train her his way; use her as he pleased. As yet, the blue skinned pair had failed to discover she existed. Scar would keep her hidden, a secret, win her loyalty, and cooperation, be ready when they sensed her.

Willow, she calls herself now. Okay. You be Willow, little darling. And you will be mine. If you want to rebel against authority, it's to my advantage. You will be my slave...I have work for you.

As for Lee; he'd better not tell. I'll fix him, if he betrays me.

Lee entered the barn to wake the girl. Scar had directed her to a stall for the night. He quickly gave them their chores: Lee to slop the pigs; Willow to collect the eggs from in the trees.

This morning, she and I feast on omelets first, alone. Then I will take her behind the fence, and teach her how to play, like the Overseers did the young females of the past.

****

As it echoed through the prehistoric jungle, Peek was the first to hear the scream. A second later, E-ri too lifted his head.

That was a female! But...my sense of her is confused. Both the girls are with us, here in the garden.

With his mind, the boy went searching; found the unschooled thoughts, and a vivid picture of the situation: a young girl; a look-a-like; the spitting image of Nitha, except for subtle differences only he could sense... She was older.

So...here is the other one. Brad's girl.

E-ri shivered at what he saw, and felt.

A vicious hair worm was at her throat, waving expectantly, seeking entrance into the terrified face. It latched on to her lip, and the helpless victim screamed silently, a second time.

E-ri transmitted the image to the mind of the small black boy beside him.

"Go!" Peek forcefully ordered, when he understood the need. "I have this. I can protect Thea and Nitha, just as well as you. Go! Hurry!"

****

Willow knew to gather the eggs from beneath the chicken's wings, but some of them left what they lay in the hollows of trees and depressions in the grass.

Why must they put them in such crazy places? They look like stones, on the ground....

She leaned closer, to examine an odd, square-shaped egg, half covered by lizard-like scales. Suddenly, there were snakes all around her, slithering through the grass. Willow dropped her basket, and slowly backed away. They slid across her knees, as if they sought even the small morsel she might hold in her hand.

For a minute, Willow remained calm, remembering instructions she'd read in a book. But when the creepy hair worm dropped to her shoulder, from the tree branch above, and began waving before her face, hissing threateningly, her fear surfaced. When it latched to her lip, a terrified scream was the involuntary, and immediate reaction.

Oh, help! It's trying to get in my mouth!

Willow's screams, from then on, were in her mind; she didn't dare voice them aloud.

With both hands, she tried to pull the thing off, but it was attached too tenaciously, and wouldn't budge.

Then suddenly, beside her, a blue/white blur appeared, with a burning stick of firewood in his hand. At first she thought he too was attacking, meant to sear her in the face, but the hissing worm, or snake, whatever it was, abruptly let go of her lip, and fell lifeless at their feet.

Too shocked to move, Willow sat there on her knees, snakes crawling over her, taking in her liberator 's features in astonishment.

He towered two inches above her, and she was tall for her age; he about a year older; at least eight. In appearance, her exact opposite; she darkly tanned with jet black hair and brown eyes; he so fair skinned his complexion appeared pale blue. His blond-white curls were cut to just below the ears, and the blue eyes had a vertical slit for the opening pupil in the center. They stared back at her, as if seeing into her very soul, and took her breath away.

Stunned, both by his sudden arrival, and his appearance, Willow remained immobile, not realizing she was still in danger.

He yanked her up, roughly, from the patch of ground where she knelt, lifted her into his arms with ease. He was strong, the embodiment of a shining knight, which made her shiver. Any other seven year old girl would have been enamored, but not worldly wise Willow...surely not! Yet somehow, her heart was doing flip flops.

Without her awareness, they were suddenly in the crotch of the tree, above the spot where they had just been moments before. She had no idea how they had gotten there.

He let her go, sat back, his eyes taking her in, wonderingly, as if she were some apparition or a marble image of someone he'd seen before. Under the shadow of the tree leaves, the whites of his eyes seemed to faintly glow...questioning with every glance.

Finally, he spoke:

"If the hair worm ever enters inside you, it takes your life. The death throws are excruciating. Even Gem cannot heal such a condition..."

A vision passed through her mind, of a small piglet being consumed, by a mass of small wiggling hair worms, tearing at its flesh, eating it from the inside out. Willow gagged.

The picture faded; silence followed.

He seemed to lose interest, scanning the trees around them. Willow finally ventured to speak.

"Thank you..." His attention returning to her, he shrugged, as if it was no big deal. "Who are you?" she asked. "I haven't seen you before...only Lee...and Scar."

"Scar's been hiding you?" he observed, as if the very fact was wrong.

Willow nodded.

"I am E-ri. Your lip is bleeding..."

He reached out and touched the spot.

Two unexpected things happened immediately: one, her injury abruptly closed, and secondly, his lip began bleeding in the same spot. She might have thought she had imagined it, for the puncture was gone seconds later, except for the words that followed.

"There. See? All better."

In this new world Willow had entered, nothing unusual would surprise her. Her knight in shining armor could heal. She grinned.

"You have healing powers?"

He shrugged nonchalantly, again.

"Time for you to meet Momma, Gem," E-ri decided, and suddenly, they were in a dome-shaped tent treehouse. A woman with similar skin coloring, had her back to them, and was bending over a large pot of bubbling stew on a small brazier.

"How many times have I told you, E-ri," the woman scolded quietly, without turned about. "Not to jump in when I am using the hot brazier inside? You could accidently knock it over, and set the place on fire."

When the woman did turn around, she was the spitting image of E-ri, except he had less curves, and she was slimmer.

"Well, what have we here? This is not Nitha."

Willow was getting very tired of being mistaken for Nitha.

"No, Momma. And, she has not been mind taught..."

"Nor is she at all acquainted with telepathy..."

He nodded. "I found her in the barnyard. I think, she's the missing one."

"No doubt. Scar thought he could hide her from us...any idea how he came by her?"

"I read her mind...sorry Momma. It was just to gain information. There is still a portal open out in the ocean..."

"Ah." The woman nodded at this information. "Forgiven. I will send Loni to investigate. Leave the girl with me. I will educate her. And..." she added, as he turned to go. "Call the others for lunch. Send the new man to Scar, as he has now lost a worker. He can also feed him, if he is so inclined."

E-ri grinned; then was gone.

Chapter 12

Loni had given Brad the barest of education in mind schooling, teaching him to project his thoughts, and to receive those of others, so he could follow along with family conversations, but the man wasn't good at it. He thought it was foolish, and therefore wouldn't concentrate. Brad often forgot, and spoke aloud, at the most inopportune times. He was a difficult man to control, when stealth was required.

The creature belongs with the farm animals; he is so noisy!

Loni had resolved, even before the finding of Willow, to give him to Scar. In agreement with Gem, he would replace both the children, Lee and Willow, with Brad. A grown man should be able to do twice as much work as any small boy.

So, that afternoon, Brad was sent to muck stalls, while Willow went to the gardens, and Lee joined Loni hunting wild game. As it worked out, Brad never knew until much later, that Willow had joined them, the lunch shifts being staggered; the children eating apart from the adults, and Brad remaining to sleep in the barn that second night.

When the man did come to sleep with the family, Loni deliberately kept Willow up, sending her to be company for E-ri on night watch.

Loni suspected Brad was a rough father, and he wanted none of that in his new world.

****

At first, Scar was livid at losing his young work force.

"Why do you deny me female help?" he demanded aloud, for Loni had never been able to get him to use mind talk. "What's the difference, male or female? They work the same, and...a female looks better, and feels...soft..."

Scar knew the reason, and Loni reminded him why, by sending a memory picture, of tiny infant Thea, his own daughter, confined, helpless, under the rock cairn, screaming in distress.

"Are you never going to forgive me? Must I pay for that the rest of my life?"

But Loni knew, he wasn't wrong in changing the order of things. He had seen in Scar's mind his plans for Willow, and he knew the Almighty had thwarted the perversion before it began.

So, Loni felt no guilt putting his two worst workmen together. They were both headstrong, and would neutralize the dreadful tendencies of each other. Loni ignored Scar, and left what he felt for the man, undeclared.

****

It had been five years since Scar had climbed the ladder from the domes, with his sack of chicks and piglets. Loni complained, but right from the first, Scar had the control. He wouldn't share meat until he had a larger store of stock. Even though Loni had helped set up the farmyard, at the expense of holding off building other more important structures, Scar only gave leftovers from his own butchering, and not until he had plenty, did he ever kill anything large. Loni always shared his wild kills, but not Scar.

Over time, Scar's menagerie expanded.

His first cow had come along the path fleeing a Tyrannosaurus. The toddling two year old, Lee, used to enjoy swinging through the trees in Scar's wake; he followed Scar everywhere. This day he was with him.

It was the first time the boy displayed his mental talent, his ability to control the wild animals of this above world, by suggestion. The tiny baby boy compelled the predator to turn away. Ever after, Lee worked at Scar's side.

The man caught that first wild cow, heavy with calf, led it to a cave to keep it safe, and later, brought it to their barrier enclosed compound. Scar rewarded the boy with a jug of milk.

Unfortunately, Lee was for sharing his gift with his brothers, and sisters; Gem discovered them, and now, years later, only because he had way too much to use himself, Scar traded milk for garden produce.

Next, Scar found the bull, in a treeless field by the lake, grazing in tall quack grass, almost up to its shoulders. He enticed the beast home with a gourd filled with wild oats.

Later, Scar found that the lake was not a fresh water body, but an ocean, beneath which was an underwater jump port, through which came the most unusual sea creatures, to supplement their diet.

If it had not been for Lydia, they would not have realized how to cook the crab and lobster. Having been raised near the ocean, she knew the crustaceans must be submerged alive in hot boiling water, or the diners would become deathly ill.

Reluctantly, Scar gave way to this wisdom, rather than risk eating them raw.

Also, the goats that had followed Scar up the ladder, multiplied rapidly. Grouse, turkey, geese, ducks, even some parrot and Myna birds flew in to join his domestic chickens.

Now, Scar had that first cow, a bull, and four milking heifers, two of which he had just bred again. He had fowl of all kinds, eggs, pork and beef, fish, sheep and goat, with plenty of both cow and goat's milk.

Often these were joined by rabbits, squirrel, snakes, and mice, taking refuge from the larger predators. They came and went; Scar couldn't confine some of them...but he would gladly eat them.

By the time the fruit trees, and vegetable gardens, began to yield, Scar had way too much meat. The only alternative was to share. As the young ones began to grow, along with their veracious appetites, all were eating well.

But Scar demanded, every meat morsel be earned. Caring for the pens and stock was constant work, so were the gardens, and orchards. To continue to eat, the young ones were taught work was as essential as nourishment.

The thorn barriers, raised first around the stock animals, was expanded, to keep out the wild life, and to close in the birds, or they would take to the skies again. They didn't dare set any livestock to forage in the fields; a cow was a mere morsel to Tyrannosaur Rex, and wild cats preyed upon human and animal alike.

Loni set a guard at night, scheduled the workforce; he had the intelligence; the perception; the insight! And somehow...Scar found he was no longer controlling the group. Loni and Gem had the young ones compliance and agreement; they obeyed without question.

Scar felt the stupid one; a simple laborer. It was like they had stepped back into the days of the Overseers.

So Scar again became the minion, inferior; the blue race, the Leaders, influential and privileged, and the dark skinned Neanderthal resented it keenly.

****

He hated them all! And now, he was saddled with this mindless human from another world.

Well, he'll work twice as hard. I'll make sure of that!

It was obvious the man couldn't read inner thoughts, and as far as Scar was concerned, that was good. Brad wouldn't see what was coming. If Scar wouldn't ever be given a female, at least a male could be made to suffer, he would make this man's life as miserable as possible.

He grinned fiendishly, thinking of things he and Galar had done in the past. He remembered how cruel the pair had been when Gem had been their prisoner. This man would be easy...

Oh, what I couldn't do during the night time...

Trouble was, Loni had said the man wasn't to sleep in the slaughter house, anymore; he'd eat and sleep with the others, in the common housing unit.

But I've got him in the daytime! He can complain to Loni all he wants about my treatment.

Chapter 13

It was the wee hours after midnight, when all were awakened by the stir in the room, then the lighting of a lamp. Brad moaned, rejecting the disturbance, rolled over, covering his head, so he wouldn't have to see or listen.

I thought sleeping here would be quieter; they said it would be safer. Surely, it isn't time to get up yet.

He had finally gotten to sleep. Scar had worked him brutally, long after sundown, as if punishing him, because Loni had taken his junior slave-labor away.

Well, that wasn't my fault! The old...whatever he is! You needn't take it out on me.

Brad understood Lee had been assigned to Scar previously. And one other, a girl. As yet, he hadn't seen her.

Poor kids! I wonder if they were dragging, as bad as I am.

His aching muscles were keeping him awake, even now.

"Jewel!" Brad started at the sharpness in Gem's tone; he never expected her to speak aloud. "Jewel!"

He realized the blue skinned woman was speaking to the only other adult female of the group. Jewel was standing in a far corner, facing into the wall.

Gem moved up behind her.

"What is wrong with you? Turn around..." There was a silent space, then Gem continued. "Say it out loud. Don't try to mind talk. Tell me what is wrong. Did you have a nightmare?"

"No...speak...long...a...leeze. Can't...stand...under!"

The woman, Jewel, was slurring dreadfully, almost as if she were drunk; barely understandable.

Gem chuckled at her weird answer, then became deadly serious.

"You can't understand?"

Jewel gave a slight nod toward the wall.

"Turn around," Gem ordered, softly.

The dark haired woman in the nightshift, finally turned, like some mechanical robot, in jerking movements, to face the blue. Gem continued to probe the mind of her friend.

"You are...dreaming?"

"Not! Afraid."

"Afraid of what? Who?"

No answer.

"You...okay?"

A jerk of her head, to the left. Gem took this to be a negative.

"Afraid of what, Jewel?" Gem challenged, a second time.

"Man. New man..."

Brad frowned, and sat up, suddenly taking interest.

What did I ever do to her?

"Why?" questioned Gem.

"No...speak...long...a...leeze."

By now, all the children were wide awake and sitting up. From a far corner eight year old E-ri spoke aloud. He was grinning from ear to ear at the antics of the two women.

"Her mind is confused, Momma Gem."

"I know," Gem returned quietly. "This isn't funny. It's serious!"

Then to Jewel again. "Open your mouth." The darker woman obeyed. "Stick out your tongue."

Once again, she complied, but the tongue refused to stay straight.

"Raise your arms." Jewel lifted only one, then dropped it.

Gem took Jewel by the shoulders, a hand on each, facing the confused woman.

"Watch her thoughts for me, E-ri," ordered Gem. "And show me what you see."

"'k Momma."

"Jewel! Again...stick out your tongue!" The organ moved to the right.

"She thinks it's straight."

Gem nodded at E-ri's observation.

This whole process puzzled Brad. It was as if Gem were sight impaired, and needed confirmation of what was happening in front of her. As if, E-ri was acting as her eyes.

Sitting there, intently watching, Brad hadn't realized Storm had moved up beside him on his bed, until the boy answered his thought.

"She is, and sees through E-ri."

Weird! Absolutely creepy.

But, Brad's attention was quickly drawn back to the two adult women, and the eight year old boy.

"What's wrong with her, Momma Gem?" asked E-ri.

"She's having a stroke."

"That's bad?"

"Can be. But, I think I've caught it on time. If I fix it now...must dissolve the clot. Go get Loni. I'll need his energy; it's still dark..."

"Poppa is...?"

"On guard near the Hydra chasm. Don't jump, E-ri. When it's dark, our energy depletes too quickly, and we need all we have."

E-ri turned, ran for the entrance, lifted the flap, and was gone, moving so fast, almost as if he'd vanished into thin air.

"Momma Gem..." probed a tentative voice. It was Thea. "I help?"

Gem shook her head.

A second voice joined in. Though she spoke hesitantly, it was the first time Brad had heard Nitha speak more than two words. He definitely knew now, this wasn't his daughter. Willow spoke well, and with confidence, when she argued her point.

"Mom...ma...I...we...are...afraid."

"Everything will be fine," Gem consoled. "Thea cuddled her," she ordered, quietly. "Your Momma will be okay."

So, Jewel is Nitha's mother?

The two tiny five year old girls went into each other's arms. And when they did, it was as if the room lost some of its apprehension.

"Storm is afraid, too," offered the small black boy.

"Not!" declared Storm, vehemently.

Brad laughed.

But Peek unabashedly admitted: "But, I am..."

Soberly, Gem observed. "It is not unmanly for boys to cuddle..."

Storm and Peek looked gravely at each other, then hesitantly moved across the room until they were together, and when they were in a huddle, Storm was the one to offer a second solution.

"We will pray, Momma Gem."

"Good. As our powers come from the Maker, we must always ask His help in these matters."

Lifting the entrance flap, E-ri stepped in, and hearing the last words, commented.

"And also, we never use our gifts for evil, only for good," he recited, as if this phrase was the finish of the other, and it had been drilled into their heads, constantly.

Loni came in behind him, tall and thin, an adult duplicate of the son. The blue man appeared to know exactly what was required of him. He immediately went to Gem.

"You left Lee and the girl to guard out there all alone?"

Brad missed the answer, as it was in mind talk, and he couldn't follow its rapidity.

Next, together with Gem, Loni guided Jewel back to sit on her bed. E-ri joined his foster brothers in the prayer circle.

Weird. They pray? I never even think to pray when there's trouble. I've always taken care of myself. As far as I'm concerned, if there was a God, where was He when I lost my wife?

Chapter 14

They first lit the dome structure with every form of light they had within it: candles; radon lamps like those used by miners. Then, Loni and Gem lay down on their backs side by side, with the unfortunate, Jewel, on the other side of Gem.

Brad felt he needed to give them privacy, so he did his best not to watch openly, laying down, himself, on his side, and feigning sleep.

The children were silent, still in a huddle, E-ri and the girls joining the other boys. When he did look at them, Brad was amazed. A light rainbow haze of light overshadowed them, above, and all around them.

Is prayer usually visible in this world?

When Brad looked at Loni, the man appeared to have dropped off to sleep, exhausted, as if all energy had escaped his body. Fear passed through Brad, an uncomfortable feeling of a malignant, unfamiliar spirit in the room.

How does a man give his energy? If this woman can do that to her man, what can she do to others?

But the next thing Brad witnessed, shocked him even more.

When Gem reached out, and took Jewel by the hand, the blue skinned woman's features began to change. The side of her face first went rigid, then, like a piece of melting plastic molding clay, one cheek began to sag; half of her lip dropped below the other; the eye above went blank, and out of focus. She now looked like something from a Zombie movie back in a theatre on planet Earth. She began mumbling incoherently.

Jewel, on the other hand, appeared at peace, comfortable again, dropping off to sleep.

Brad shivered, turned onto his stomach. He couldn't watch anymore; he buried his head beneath his arms.

The room seemed to have filled with a ominous dread.

The children still prayed, silently.

As the light of dawn filled the dome cover overhead with brightness from the outside, Brad could bear the suspense no longer. He turned over, to look again.

The three participants were sleeping peacefully. Gem was perfectly normal; so was Jewel, and Loni was even snoring. It was as if Brad had dreamed the whole thing.

The children too, had slipped from their knees, and slid away to their prospective corners to sleep.

For more than an hour after, Brad lay awake, pondering, wondering, whether he had imagined what had gone on.

He finally dropped off, and it was nearly noon before he awoke. His belly was then screaming for any kind of nourishment. One of the little girls had made a pot of porridge.

It wasn't until late in the evening, after his chores, that Brad realized his daughter, Willow, was among the other children. She failed to approach him, having suddenly become leery of him, and avoiding.

You really couldn't tell her apart from Nitha, and he never noticed there were two of them coming and going. Though there was two years difference, there was only a two inch variation in their height, and that could only be seen, if they stood next to each other.

****

E-ri said, they had the day off. He had asked Loni. The adults were incapacitated, due to the healing that had taken place in the night. Work was therefore suspended; everyone needed the break. Only the farm needed a worker, and that must be an adult.

The new man was appointed.

Poppa Loni was as drained of energy as Momma Gem, and even though she had been the one healed, Jewel continued to sleep the day away. This left the children at loose ends.

"Come to the Lagoon with us," suggested Thea to Nitha's look-a-like. "The boys like to show off their diving skill. They jump from the top of the waterfall."

Willow grinned, and nodded, but like Nitha, she said little, following mostly, leaving Thea to lead.

Golly, but they sure have some of the same mannerisms! Both so quiet.

Already, Willow had mastered the vine to vine travel through the trees. She fit in well. But, E-ri was her constant shadow; as the weakest link, he appeared afraid she'd be hurt.

When the girls arrived in the sheltered Lagoon at the base of the fifty foot falls, the other boys were already, daringly, diving off a jutting rock about fifteen foot from the top. E-ri took his station in a nearby tree, guardian always, of the group.

While Storm, Peek, and Lee dove into the foaming depth, E-ri watched; he always had, though Thea knew, he often went off alone, and jumped, not from the shorter ledge, but from the very top. He was eight; the other boys only six; he was old enough to be on his own, and besides, he had the power to teleport; the others did not.

The girls took their place in the branches of a tree near the sandy shore, beneath, on the opposite side of the water spray at the base.

"Sometimes, I think, E-ri acts too grown up," Nitha observed by thought. "He never plays...with others, that is."

Willow, attempting her new found skill, tried to think back an answer:

"I like him," she declared, then realized what she was confessing in this unguarded communication, and blushed a deep crimson.

Thea chuckled.

"That's okay," she reassured, to ease Willow's discomfort. "I like Storm. But the younger boys haven't matured enough to care, or even notice we are girls yet. Who do you like, Nitha?"

Shyly, Nitha grinned, and tried to verbalize her preference.

"Pee...ek!"

"Not Lee?" prompted Thea out loud.

"Too!"

"You don't have to try to speak aloud, just for my benefit, Nitha," Willow decided. "I do understand your mind talk; quite easily now. Gem is a good teacher."

Nitha agreed with a nod, and a comfortable silence followed, while they watched the antics of the boys. When the combatants disappeared for a time, Thea brought up a subject important to them all.

"You two do realize you are half sisters, don't you?"

Willow looked at her with a question in her eyes.

"What makes you come by that conclusion? Just because we look so much alike?"

"Silly," scolded Thea. "Do you not feel your bond?"

At this observation, Nitha silently nodded, and added in thought:

"We share dreams...I know you have been with me in stress situations..."

Willow shivered, as memories of vivid nightmares were triggered.

After seconds, where she pondered this reality, Willow tried to refute it.

"But...that can't be," she disagreed. "That would mean...we have a common parent. And my father has never been away from me...since...momma died..."

"So...you know basic 'birds and bees' theory?" chuckled Thea.

Willow grunted in annoyance. "Course I do. I read a lot!"

"Your dad...Brad, didn't tell you?"

"He doesn't know, I know what boys can do; he keeps me away from them. Why do you think I got curious? So, I researched it..."

The other two girls laughed out right.

"Gee whiz, anyway," Willow declared, blushing. "You guys are only five. How'd you find out, anyway?"

"Well," stated Thea, thought projecting, matter-of-factly sending an image along with her words. "We do have a barnyard..."

"And the power to reason," finished Thea. "What's good with the animals; same goes for intelligent, upright walkers..."

"Sheesh!" Willow exclaimed aloud.

After a time, she went back to the original subject, and sat brooding.

"If you are right," she finally stated, slowly. "That means...Jewel...would have to be..."

"Your mother!" finished Thea.

"No way!" Willow declared emphatically, rejecting that obvious conclusion. "My mom's name was Lydia..."

Thea chuckled, delighted she was right. "Poppa Loni gives us pet names. Gem isn't Momma Gem's real name either. It's Gemma, and he only calls Lydia, Jewel, because...when we were younger, we couldn't say her real name..."

Willow hardly read the last of that mind message. All she could do was shake her head in astonishment. She sat there, silent and tense for a time, quietly absorbing the fact...she had just found her mother!

"But...does she know?" she finally asked, incredulous.

"Oh, I'm quite sure she does," Thea observed. "Last night, she made it obvious she knows who Brad is...and fears him!"

"But...why doesn't he recognize her?" exploded Willow, aloud.

"She's changed a lot," Thea volunteered. "And...your Poppa...is kinda...slow."

Willow snorted, derisively, realizing her new friend had reasoned the obvious. "Tell me about it!"

"Well..." suggested Thea. "We'd best let the elders work it out among themselves... Hey! Want to go for a swim?"

"Sure." Willow was always game for a swim. "Oh, say. Don't tell the boys just yet, okay?"

The other two girls giggled.

"E-ri has already figured it out," Thea revealed. "Not much gets by him. And I don't think the other three are stupid either, but we'll keep your secret as long as needed...at least, 'till your dumb male parent catches on."

Chapter 15

Oh, I have just had enough of this!

Brad had lain there for hours mulling over the facts of his situation. Long past, the even breathing of the others signaled they were asleep, and the large dome-like tent had gone silent, he had been stewing. Now, even the wild life, in the distance, had ceased their grumblings. It was close to dawn.

Loni was off somewhere, watching as sentry. Brad didn't know what the man expected to attack, other than the wild prehistoric creatures of this world, but still, he always went out to watch, or sent another. Tonight Loni would not be a problem, and Brad had just had enough of the man's constant control.

The only time Brad saw his daughter was at night, when he was too tired to interact civilly with her. At meals, she placed herself with the children; Loni was always beside Brad.

Willow had changed; avoiding him, always silently talking, and giggling with the other two girls, or with the boy, E-ri, as he sat between Brad and her. Brad couldn't follow their fast mind talk, and when he voiced a comment, aloud, it was usually disregarded. Sometimes, Brad wondered if this was deliberate, to train him to mind talk. But the father craved verbal conversation, and would have none of it, so was left out.

There is never a moment where I can privately converse with my daughter!

What is this? A conspiracy to keep us apart?

And Scar? A monkey man; if he is a man at all... What right has he to be my boss? To load me down with work, so I don't have a minute to rest or think! Scar never gives me a moment's reprieve from sun up until sunset. I'm not a slave!

They all drove him to distraction, constantly working, with never a break; always silent talking to each other; leaving him out of the loop.

Not putting up with this anymore!

****

Willow swallowed a gasp as a rough hand, smelling of pig manure, covered her mouth; another encircling her waist, lifted her from her mat. At first she thought it was Scar, but then realized, this was her father, but...he could only mean harm, grabbing her in this way.

He lifted her violently from the floor, carrying her bodily from the room. Though she knew this was her father, who was usually so noisy, tonight he was being stealthy, and careful.

What is he up to?

Willow ceased to struggle, knowing it was pointless, because, if Brad meant to punish for something she'd done, she wasn't strong enough to fight him.

He didn't put her down until they were on the ground, far beneath the tent, and a good distance away, so they could not be heard. Then, pulling her along with him, he continued through the forest.

Finally, he released her.

Willow knew, all she had to do was call out to E-ri, and he'd come to her rescue, but she decided to see what her father was up to first. She remained silent.

They had not had a chance to talk since arriving here.

It's time Daddy has a chance to get what is bothering him off his chest.

****

Jewel rose up, suddenly awake and aware. It didn't take long for her to locate the reason for her rousing. One of the children was missing, and...so was Brad.

It meant only one thing.

He's leaving...and taken my Willow with him. Just when I'm getting to know her, at last.

That was when Jewel made her first mistake.

She decided to follow, but...went alone, sneaking away, without the knowledge of the others.

****

E-ri came awake, the silent dome structure like a sounding bell to him. The consciousness of Willow was away from his awareness, and...that wasn't right.

Something is wrong!

Then he knew. The memories of the three missing occupants still hung in the air.

He stood to follow, but another had the same alertness. A quiet thought voice arrested his movements, brought him up short, cautioning him.

"Leave them, E-ri," Gem gently reasoned. "They all need time to work out their problems."

The eight year old obeyed, dropping again to his mat, silently objecting, yet not in rebellion.

"They are defenseless... They will be hurt..."

"Sometimes, people need that to learn, E-ri," Gem counseled. "We will watch from afar. Don't worry so...the Maker is their protector. He brought them here..."

E-ri knew to what Gem eluded, how a Higher Intelligence seemed to guide all their steps. Since his conception, that loving Being had oversaw all their smallest daily interactions, giving them the talents to cope, working out everything to a certain end...even to Willow's coming. All because Momma Gem was their constant prayer cover...talking always with that Entity.

It told her things, prepared her...showed her visions of future events.

E-ri lay down, and soon was again fast asleep.

****

When Brad felt they had put enough distance between them, and the camp, he stopped with his daughter to tell her of his plans.

"We are getting out of here," he whispered. "Going home."

"How are you going to do that?" Willow demanded by thought. "You know Loni says the Portals only go one way."

"Speak aloud!" he fired back in annoyance. "You know, I can't follow along."

"You could, if you tried harder. If I can, so can you."

"Loni lies to us. He wants to keep us apart...keep us from leaving."

"No, he doesn't! I can see in his mind. The Portals we came through only go one way..."

"The hell! He told you that?"

"No. Loni's personal, mental deliberation. They can't lie during reflection. They can't even tell an untruth. Momma Gem showed me that!"

"That's probably a lie, too!"

"It's true!"

"Oh, they've got you so brainwashed, you can't even think straight.! We are leaving this place!"

"What if I don't want to leave?"

"I'm your father! You do as I say! Don't you see, why they want you to stay? They need girls! There are too many boys!"

"Oh, Poppa! Why do you think they accept you, then?"

Brad laughed bitterly.

"Oh, I'm just a slave! Of little use, but to work for Scar."

"Daddy..." she pleaded. "I...like it here. I have friends...like a family."

Brad was deaf to her entreaty; he would not even consider her words. He had his own opinion.

"I came down here to search for your mother's body. It isn't here, so we're going. And that's that!"

"Maybe..." Willow hesitantly offered. "You can't see...what's in front of your nose?"

Brad's temper flared.

"You've sure gotten uppity since you got in with others your own age. Who do you think you are, giving me correction? I'm your father. I've taught you everything you know..."

"Not everything...I learn from books..."

"You read too much! And what did you mean? I can't see what's in front of me. You think I should forget her, and take another woman? Oh, now, that would please them just fine! I see where this is going. They put that in your head; didn't they? Well, you're just a kid; what do you know?"

Brad went silent, fuming.

The little brat knows nothing about physical attraction! The woman is ugly, even if her name is Jewel. What a misnamed creature...how could I ever want her after Lydia's compliant nature? Man!...Why does this other woman have to seem so giving?...Just like Lydia...

If Willow had really learned to read minds, and Brad's thoughts were unguarded, it would have been obvious to her, all she had to do was wait, and all would work out...if they stayed in the commune. But the child had also been taught not to invade the privacy of the mind, and therefore, did not read her parent's musings.

In despair, Willow too went silent, having learned from previous experience, it was pointless to argue, when her father had set his mind to reason against her wishes.

Deciding he had won the disagreement, Brad grabbed his daughter's arm, and took off again through the trees. The path was unfamiliar to Willow, and with no other choice, she went along, though reluctantly.

****

Jewel caught up to the pair just as the sun came up over the tree tops. She was upon them, before Brad even realized, he was being followed.

To make certain she had his full attention, Jewel grabbed at his arm, and held to it tenaciously. He swung viciously toward her, let go of his daughter, and raised his fist to strike Jewel. When he saw who it was, he growled at her. Then, he back handed her hard, across the cheek.

As Jewel fell to the mulch of the forest floor, Brad stood over her, straddling her, threateningly. She could have raised a knee, and sent an excruciating blow to his jewels. All he was wearing were soft animal skin shorts. But she chose not to. Instead, she lay defenseless on her back, looking up at him with suppressed wrath in her eyes.

"She's my daughter!" Brad hissed venomously. "You can't have her! I'm taking her out of here."

"Mine...too!" stuttered Jewel.

"Like hell! Just when did YOU give birth to her?"

"Before Chemo...seven...year's...ago."

Brad's jaw dropped. He frowned; his manner wilted.

Behind him, Willow grinned, and moved away.

It is time for the final battle. At last!

****

Brad reached down, and offered the woman a hand up. He at once regretted having hit her.

She is a helpless, handicapped woman. I would never have done something like this to Lydia. What's wrong with me?

He stared into the expressive brown eyes, now just below his. They were filled with tears.

Brad had never had a chance, before this, to look directly in the woman's eyes. They were disconcerting...just like Lydia's had been... They had always showed him his guilt.

"Don't know...me. Do...you?"

His jaw went slack again, as recognition dawned on him.

"Lydia?" he whispered breathlessly. "It can't be..."

He dropped his eyes, suddenly self-conscious.

"So...mean...to...Wil...low!" she reproved.

He never had been able to stand her disapproval. Brad stepped away; sat down under a nearby tree to catch his breath, and get his bearings.

She stood quietly over him, the roles now reversed, while he thought things over. Finally he spoke, his voice pleading like an errant small boy, caught doing something so horrendous the act was disapproved of.

"I tried to raise her the way you would, but I had to be not just father, but provider...and mother, too. I missed you so much. I was...angry, so angry...hurt...that you would leave me. And, what they did to you...all to lose you in the end...they..."

"Who?" she demanded.

For a woman with a speech impediment, she chose her words wisely. She was good at getting her point across. The past seemed so pointless to hang to now.

He decided to turn the scrutiny away from himself.

"Why do you stay with these people?" he challenged. "Why do you let them control you, like they do?"

She huffed indignantly.

"No diff...rant...then...you!"

He swallowed hard at that.

Is that what she remembers of me? I was heavy handed? I had to be...to get her through all she had to endure. She never would have made it, if I hadn't been firm.

Was I cruel to her?

"Lon...ee...Gem...I...die...if...not...for...Gem..."

"I realize that, but..."

"Twice!" hissed Lydia. "She...save...heal!"

In his mind, Brad remembered the last healing, and was humbled. Ashamed, he dropped his eyes.

"You...not...know...how...bad...it...was! How...much...I...owe...them!"

"I'm sorry," was his meek return.

"Not leaving! Best...here!"

He nodded, finally agreeing.

In the near distance, a scream rent the air.

Turning, Brad at last realized, Willow was gone. He leapt to his feet, as Jewel turned in fear toward the sound. The man turned, and ran frantically, when the second scream rang out.

Chapter 16

As a reflex, Willow screamed when she saw the huge Tyrannosaurus towering above her. If she had been silent, he never would have seen her. Without thinking, she turned and ran, revealing her position. The beast came thundering after her.

The second scream came when the ground beneath her feet gave way. Next thing she knew, she was falling, plunging into a darkened, rank smelling cavern.

Willow cracked her head hard against the rock shelf. Her neck whipped back; head bounced, and the world fled away.

****

Arriving in the place where he thought the screams originated, Brad saw nothing of Willow. He turned, and searched the opposite direction. There lumbering down upon him was a huge monster of a dinosaur. It failed to see him, intent upon seeking out its original prey.

He sidestepped to avoid the creature, and never saw the fissure. Next thing, he was dropping, the sifting sediment sliding into the hole with him. Down, down, he plunged, until he was caught by the limb of a root system. He stopped short with a jerk; then the branch cracked, broke off, and he was deposited, with a bone shattering jar on sandy soil of a rock shelf.

For a moment, he lay there stunned. Then he roused himself enough to examine his person. It appeared, he was unhurt. Only his ego was bruised.

Should have seen that...

He lay on his back, looking far up at the hole he'd made far above. Lydia's head appeared, and he yelled a warning to her.

"Watch out for the T-rex!"

"Are...you...hurt?"

"Don't appear to be. Have you seen Willow? First, where's the monster?"

"Gone!...ran...past!"

"Okay." Brad sat up. "We have to find Willow. Is she down here? Can you see her?"

A moment of silence followed, while both parents looked about, he from below; she from on top. Finally, Jewel pointed to another shelf to his right, just below him, but on the opposite side.

"Far...ther...down...ledge!"

Brad rolled to his belly, peering over into the chasm, that seemed to drop eternally, beneath him. He shivered, as he realized how close they'd all come to being dashed on hidden rocks, or vanishing forever.

Willow too, had been caught, by the out cropping of a stone slab, but she hadn't fared so well as he. By the position of her body, Brad knew she had been hurt grievously.

"Go get help, Lydia. I'll try to get down to her..."

****

Nitha awoke screaming, then her fear turned to sobs. Thea understanding quickly, this wasn't just a nightmare, rolled over, and gathered her into her arms. She had received the same dream.

Gem stepped into the sleeping area, carrying a small lit brazier, on which was a bubbling pot of gruel. She too appeared forewarned of the developing tragedy, though she remained calm.

"Willow is hurt," Thea declared in mind talk. "They have fallen...way down..."

Gem nodded, without commenting, and carefully set her burden down.

Lee came pounding into the hut, the other two boys right behind him. All were still wet from their morning swim.

"E-ri says, something's wrong!"

"We know. No need to panic," Gem returned quietly. "Sit down. We eat. Then we'll help them from here."

Her composure did much to alleviate the children's fear. Nitha swiped at her tears, and sat up.

"How?" asked Lee with concern, dropping to his knees, in preparation for the meal.

"Eat first," ordered Gem, gently.

****

Using his arms, Brad had managed to lower himself from his shelf, and swing across to where Willow lay unconscious. He now lay on the silt covered, hard rock ledge with the injured girl in his arms. Mercifully, she was not awake to feel the excruciating pain that would have been hers in a cognizant state. Her body was bashed, broken, and bruised in many places, from tumbling against rocks that jutted out from the walls.

Brad willingly took the blame.

This is all my fault!

If he hadn't taken her from the sleep dome; hadn't tried to take her away.

For that matter, if she hadn't followed me here, to this place, in the first place...if I hadn't left her alone up there...if I'd not taken her with me; left her home with a Nanny...She would have been a contented, happy girl, playing back there with friends; oblivious of all this. Innocent! Like she should have been!

Geesh! So many things I could have done differently. Why didn't I?

Now, I am about to lose her. Forever! What will I do without her?

For the first time in her life, Brad was finally seeing his daughter as what she was. Not an adult, but a little girl of seven; a slight, fragile female he'd treated, all her life, as a servant to follow his bidding...a piece of property, he meant to train properly.

Gosh! What a fool I've been.

Have I ever really shown her love?

Brad trembled with the shock, and the regret of it.

I may never get the chance to, now.

He cuddled Willow close in his arms, rubbed his cheek against her smooth dark hair. It was wet with her own blood, yet it smelled of her scent, and felt soft to his touch. Her face; the skin, was soft, silken.

Oh, God! I'm sorry. I'll never abuse her again. I promise!

Tears welled in his eyes; one travelled unnoticed down his cheek, into the hair of his tiny girl. Brad gasp with anguish, trying to hold back.

Why hadn't he seen what he had, instead of searching for something he thought he'd lost? This treasure had always been right here.

And Lydia...it had been nothing but Lydia...a dream of the past, exaggerated.

Did God keep her from me...'till I would accept the treasure I had?

Like a voice in his mind, Brad felt the comforting presence of someone else...not like the telepathic thoughts of the blue skinned race, but different...something...all encompassing.

Is that Loni? Or Gem? No?

It's different. Not like the telepath's thoughts...

Is that an answer? Is...are you...my Maker?

"Oh, man!" moaned Brad aloud. It was as if he were being caressed by an immense, benevolent hand. He began to sob.

"God...if you are listening," he whispered. "I promise...if you spare her...I'll be a better man. I'll be attentive...to both of them! I'll protect them...with my life! If you'll...just help me..."

Brad wept openly, great sobs wracking his frame. All the years of pent up rage, and rebellion washed away...and when it was over, the man lay quiet beside his unconscious daughter, submissive.

****

Up above, Lydia, the one called Jewel, watched silently. She knew what was happening. For many years, she had prayed for just such an encounter. She had never expected to witness it.

A long time ago, she had learned the one talent given her, to read the body language of others. When you are limited in what you can say, it helped to understand the motives of others.

Jewel let him cry, not disclosing her presence, until the moment was right, though she longed to hold her man, and give him comfort.

She remembered...now, how in the past, this husband had held her, as she trembled in fear of her next radiation treatment.

Even before that, when she had dreaded the cutting knife, that would remove that tumor from her brain...and maybe, leave her mindless.

Brad had been with her, comforting her...she remembered it still...

But...a whole other life had been passed between...Da, Nitha...Loni and Gem...the babies...now, somewhat grown.

Can I go back to what was before?

I can...at least, be patient...wait and see...and be loving.

It is time to forgive him...

If Brad was ready; she could accept him back.

****

"How...bad?" Jewel asked from above, jarring Brad to wakefulness.

He swiped at his tears, so she wouldn't see. Still the proud, ego oriented male. But he swallowed his pride.

She hadn't gone for help, after all. Had she been watching, all this time? Brad chose to ignore the obvious.

"Think her arm's broken; may be even her back...and there's a bad gash on her forehead. I wish I had something to at least splint her arm..."

Brad let out a startled yelp. Suddenly, crawling all over him, were dozens of tiny fat rodents. He gasped, drew back; batted at a few of them, anxiously. Yet, still, they kept coming...until, he and Willow were covered like a blanket.

"Oh...MAN! What IS this?"

It was then he noticed, among the pack, two lines, like prisoners in a chain gang, carrying dead branches in their teeth.

"What...the...HECK?"

From up above, Jewel laughed aloud.

"Lee!" she exclaimed, gleefully.

"What?"

"Lee! He...control...wild...ones..."

"How...the heck, can he do that?"

"Don't...ques...tion!...He...tell...them...bring!"

"You're kidding me!"

"Try...take."

Obediently, Brad reached out tentatively, took one of the branches by the end, and tried to pull it from the tiny creatures. With ease, they relinquished it. He reached for the second. It too came away without objection.

The first branch was just the right length, but the second too long. Brad quickly snapped it off. He realized, he now had two splints.

"Wow! Now, all I need is some rope..."

He looked about him; the rodents were gone.

Moments later, his small helpers were back, dragging between them a long length of strong fibrous vine.

Brad laughed with amazement.

"Five year old Lee is doing this?" he demanded, incredulous.

"He...do...since...three!"

"Wow! That's why, he's so good with the animals."

By the time Brad had Willow's arm in a splint, E-ri appeared above, beside Jewel.

Bran was so speechless, he went to mind talk.

"Did you send for the others?" he asked the woman above.

E-ri answered for her:

"We watch your back, Mr. human father."

The grin on E-ri's face turned quickly to serious, as next, he was in the hole beside the man and the girl, assessing their injuries.

"Willow need's Gem. Extensive healing this time," he declared gravely, then cautiously lifting the battered girl in his arms, disappeared from sight with her, leaving her parents to fend for themselves.

At Brad's feet, a long vine rope appeared, again compliments of the small pack of helpers, and their controller, Lee. Brad found it was enough to make a rope ladder, and a lasso to toss it to Jewel. With her help, he soon, too was rescued.

But the return trip took much longer than expected. Brad had finally surrendered to the use of mind talk, as it was the most efficient way to communicate with his recently discovered partner. They had much to talk about; years to catch up with...little attention was paid to their surroundings.

If not for tiny Peek, and Lee, watching from above in the trees, the pair would certainly have had another disastrous encounter before they made it back to camp.

Chapter 17

Brad became a different man, from that day forward. Once Willow was healed, and Loni and Gem sufficiently recovered, for things to return to normal, the two men began building another family dwelling.

Eventually, it was agreed, Brad would now be responsible, not just for his own daughter and wife, but also the half daughter of Lydia and Da. Loni would be over Brad, in the function of advisor/counselor, while Gem, always would be friend, and confidant to Jewel. The Leader pair had decided to trust the family to govern their own affairs, while still being part of the overall group, sharing in both labor and produce.

Somehow, it didn't end there. Soon, the third girl, Thea, usually the voice for Nitha, spent more time with the other young ladies, then in her own dome. To ease and give privacy, to both couples, it became necessary to allot times...for sleepover's; the girls always together at one tent, or another.

And like a shadow, E-ri, too, insinuated himself, wherever the girls were. He declared, they needed protection, though it was obviously more than that. The need was admitted, and sanctioned.

After him came Peek; then, hesitantly, Storm, and last of all, Lee. Now, the children, somehow, were always all together, with a different family to sleep.

Thus, their upbringing was therefore shared.

Another change came about with this: At Loni's suggestion, Scar began to eat with the larger group at noon and evenings. Halfheartedly, he became a part of the whole.

Life went on for a few months, in pleasant harmony, and then, one day, their world changed drastically again.

****

Peek came flying into the main dome, to wake Loni early. The Elder had been sentry, by the Hydra cave, the previous night.

"Poppa...Poppa! Danger!"

Loni shot to a sitting position, wide eyed, and abruptly awake.

"Scar says, bad men came through fisherman's portal..."

"How long ago?" Loni urgently demanded, still a bit disoriented.

"They have guns!" declared Lee emphatically, storming in behind the other boy, to add his two cents to the drama. "E-ri says, come quick!"

Loni rubbed his hand across his face and jaw, to give himself time to think. He'd expected trouble for years, but not from this quarter.

If E-ri is worried, he's seen something threatening in their minds.

Loni arose quickly to follow.

****

Storm and E-ri were together, perched in a tree above the well worn path. It was rare to see these two together, as both were such loners. This fact alone, brought to Loni, the suggestion of the alarm this was causing all the boys.

Below, on the path to the barn yard, five burly soldiers, dressed in green and brown camouflage, carrying automatic rifles, side arms at their hips, were slinking single file toward the ten foot high thorn barrier, surrounding the animal housing. It was, as if they knew exactly what they were approaching; knew what was there, and whom it housed.

Loni silently wondered, how they had come by that knowledge.

In mind-talk, E-ri stated the obvious: "The farm animals are audible for miles; you simply can't hear them."

Every so often, his handicap was brought to his attention. It wasn't often, Loni forgot he couldn't hear actual sound, for life was so full of mental noise: other's thoughts, or the sounds through their ears, and your own private musings, he often thought of himself as actually hearing abundantly; to him, he wasn't deaf.

When Loni had been a boy of twelve, as a punishment for starting a devastating fire, that had cost many lives, the Overseer/Physician had poured acid down his ear channels, burning away, not only, his inner ears, but the whole outer core, leaving the boy mutilated, deaf, and mute. He had barely survived, but in so doing, he had learned a valuable lesson in endurance; and...the art of telepathy.

Loni nodded to acknowledge the observation. His son was simply explaining something that puzzled the still sleep muddled elder. He knew, it was not meant to put him down.

Loni watched the men below; they inched from tree to tree, as if they thought they weren't at all visible, but they stood out against the gold and orange foliage like a black cloud. What they were wearing was like a shout to the world.

He knew these new males were from another world, unfamiliar with their surroundings. They came from the place where Brad, Lydia, and Gem originated, as stupid as Brad had been at first, but...what to do with them? That was the question. And whether they meant to harm the commune, was a more imperative factor.

From his Gem, he had read much about such men; a cruel, vicious lot, set upon being the controllers...as Brad had been, before the Maker had seen fit to deal with him. These were males who had no capacity to love, nor show compassion. You could not expect mercy from them...like an Overseer!

Loni shivered, as if a cold draft from the past had washed over him.

He wondered:

How did they get the guns through?

That was when he noticed the packs on their backs, the trunks of gear they dragged along after themselves.

They've been planning this a long time. How? They must have some sort of communication back through the portal... Are the Overseers back? And in correlation with them?

"There is another man far ahead, watching Scar," E-ri broke into his thoughts. "He came through alone, a few days ago..."

"Why wasn't I told?"

"Scar simply laughed it off; said he'd soon die by his own stupidity. He thought, he was an Overseer; he didn't think it important."

"Well, it was!"

What was I busy at, that I didn't pick up on the other mind?

And like an answer in his thoughts, came the words: 'You are not God!'

The Maker had blinded them...for what reason?

"He must have sent a message back through..." Loni reasoned. "But, how? I thought the Portals only went one way..."

E-ri shrugged, as if Loni had expected him to answer.

"They set up camp quickly, last night. You were on the other side, by the Hydra shelf..."

"Why didn't you sense some of this?"

"First, you've ordered us: 'Kids, don't play by the ocean port!' Always, you have warned us. Vehemently! Secondly...I watch the others. My mind can only go so many places...when they split up...I'm only...eight..." he mourned contritely. "I'm sorry..."

Stricken with guilt, Loni moaned aloud. He reached out an arm, and drew the boy against him.

"I'm sorry son. I expect too much..."

E-ri grinned. "All forgiven." Then, with tongue in cheek, he asked the loaded question:

"Why didn't you, or Momma...or even Thea, sense them?"

And then, Loni remembered. The beginning of the evening had been a free night for Gem, and he. They had spent it together, before he went out to watch. Thea would have guarded her mind; E-ri gone directly to sleep. And while Loni was on guard, his thoughts were reviewing the previous pleasantry...

Oh drat! Therein lies our weakness.

E-ri giggled knowingly, but Loni simply ignored him.

That boy is far more mature, than I was at that age.

The other two boys had silently waited, while Loni and E-ri held their usual rapid-fire telepathic conference. It was something they were used to.

Loni turned to Lee, and sent him a command in mind talk.

"Lee, corner the man ahead, and send him to their camp. Don't let the stalking animal hurt him..."

E-ri grinned in anticipation, now, thrilled by the prospect of the catch.

Lee laughed delighted. "Tiger will simply play with him..."

"Storm, bring on the rain, and drive the other men back to camp. Hold them there! When they have settled down, the two of you, go help Scar with the chores. Tell him, we'll handle this from here..."

"What about Brad?"

"I'll need to confer with him first. I'll send him along later..."

Chapter 18

As she was still asleep, and he didn't want to wake her, Brad tried not to move, when Loni stepped into their sleep dome. It was their turn to spend the day alone, and he was just too comfortable, with that dark head resting against his shoulder. Private moments, with Lydia, were rare, even now, that they were scheduled.

Brad wondered at this invasion by the blue-skinned telepath; to invade their space was not like Loni. He knew how important it was to give each couple space, and had been adamant, the children not do so.

"Something serious has come up," Loni quietly informed him. "I need your expertise. Come out; talk to me...as soon as possible...when it is convenient."

It was almost an apology. Brad realize this was not an average problem, but the man's mind was closed to him.

Loni abruptly turned, and carefully vacated their quarters.

****

Sometime later, after Brad had awakened Lydia, and explained why he was leaving her. He didn't want her to think, he was abandoning her for some foolish reason. He joined Loni by the Hydra shelf look out, where they had first met.

Brad had become more proficient at two things: mind-talk, and moving through the trees quietly.

A family has been good for me...and fellowship of mind, as well.

Loni smiled, and nodded. "Indeed."

One thing that still always shook Brad, was the way Loni felt no qualms at invading his privacy. To enter a companion's mind was so easy for him, he seemed to have little regard for the right and wrong of it. Brad supposed the man needed to know the dependability of the other, and that was the surest way to assess it. Brad had learned to humble himself, to cope, and...adjust.

In Brad's mind, he had excused the habit, by the realization, he was already well known by his Maker, who probed him deeply, now, intimately, during his constant musings. If Loni shared in this intimate dialogue with his God, he never let on; more, Loni seemed pleased by it.

"So...what's so threatening?"

"Follow me..."

****

They were now in the trees above, a short distance from the animal compound, where a cleverly disguised camp site had been set up. It would have been more appropriate for the jungle of Earth, with its netting hanging from the trees, painted in greens, blacks, and tan, but here, it stood out against the autumn colored trees, and foliage.

Brad frowned, thinking: old habits die hard.

What is an army camp doing set up here?

Only in this area, was it raining; pouring absolute buckets. Suddenly, Brad realized why.

"Storm's doing?" he questioned. "To keep them stationery, while we think of a plan?" Loni nodded. "So, how many men?"

Just at that moment, a large beefy man came out of the tent. He was stripped to the waist; covered in mud. He picked up a bucket, that had filled with water, replaced it with an empty one, and carried the full one inside.

"Seven, all told...why are they here? Who are they?" questioned Loni, as if Brad should know, just because of where he came from.

Brad shook his head perplexed.

"Damned if I know!" he exploded, without thinking.

Loni hissed disapprovingly. "Language! Human!"

"Sorry..." Brad returned in thought, contritely.

He pondered a while.

"Maybe..." he speculated. "They found our empty boat...and started a search for us..."

He shook his head, rejecting the premise. "But...we were never that important! No one even knew Willow was with me...even for a young girl; I don't think they would send out Special Forces to look for her..."

"What are 'Special Forces'?"

"They are an elite force of soldiers, specially train to invade enemy territory, to execute a kill or such..."

"Why would such men come here? They are from your world, right?"

Brad nodded, exceedingly puzzled, himself.

"They are dangerous?"

"Deadly men."

"Trouble for us? Not friendly?"

"Not likely; I wouldn't be trusting them...they are here for a purpose. My guess is, to invade..."

"What do you mean by that? Take over; conquer; enslave...dominate?"

"All of that. Be on your guard. My people...the men of Earth usually subjugate what they think inferior..."

Loni nodded. "I have read of your history...the Overseers had libraries on that world."

Brad shrugged. He wasn't surprised.

"The Overseers came from there?"

"No. They came from here; invaded your world; used the females to breed..."

Disgusted, Brad reacted. "Well, I guess you can expect it to come back on you in time..."

"I did not do it..."

"Then...explain Gem. Lydia has told me of you, and Da..."

Tears formed in Loni's eyes. Then he sent Brad the most powerful impressions the human had ever experienced. Vividly, Brad felt Loni's past; all the horrific detail, and pain of it. It sped by so fast, it made him dizzy, and sick. Perhaps, if it hadn't been rapid, the viewing of it would have damaged him.

With a gasp, Brad doubled over, retching. Loni touched his shoulder, and there was equilibrium, once more.

And the Earthman knew, he would never again judge the man. Loni seldom defended himself, but when he did, he had good reason. He had taken no part in kidnapping; nor had he forced himself on Gem. Loni had been as much a prisoner as the women, and by their law, both couples had first been married.

Satisfied, and now quietly, at peace with each other, the two men sat assessing the situation. Brad was the one to finally think out the reasoning.

"They never send an invasion force first; usually, such men as these go in ahead to check things out..."

"They came through the portal..."

"Must have discovered it while searching the wreckage of the plane..."

"Well, they came well prepared...with weapons, food, disguises..."

"And devices to communicate with the outside world. They expected...no they planned for any eventuality on this side. They must have sent a probe through first. This has been going on for weeks, Loni..."

"We must stop it! More men will come! Especially, when they realize, they cannot get back..."

"Portal only goes one way?"

Loni nodded. "I will try to collapse it..."

"And what about the portal I came through?"

"Yes. And, there is also another, somewhere, that goes both ways. I have not yet found that; it is somewhere beyond the tunnels, and those are still very unstable, some impassible. I will try to collapse all portals, one at a time, but it takes great mental concentration...if I can do it at all."

"Then, that would just leave these seven to deal with..."

****

Trumack had been trained for most any situation, just never such a world as this. When he stepped through the portal, he knew that things would be alien and weird, just because humans of his world didn't even have the technology to make such a gate.

Here they were, stepping into something so foreign you could anticipate the stuff of Science Fiction...but tree trunks of purple, upside-down branches, leaves mauve and orange, a sun more tangerine copper than light yellow, and two moons with stars going out past the planet in circler rings. Not to mention the wildlife: tigers, cougars, elephants, and bears, co-existing alongside Tyrannosaurus Rex. Who knew what else was out there?

His number one man had gone through first, a day ahead of the core group. He hadn't been able to come back through, but the lowest radio wave band had carried the message. Over many hours, he had managed to describe, not only some of what was there, but what they would need to bring to the other side, and before they followed after, they all knew, this was a one way trip; the mission, to conquer the local aborigines, and establish their base.

But number one had not been able to prepare them for the vivid colors, nor the diversity of the wildlife. There had not been time to convey much more than the basics.

The shock hit their systems as they stepped through. First it was the frigid cold and grayness inside the fishery. Then, when they stepped into daylight, the shouting of color; the intense heat...the bizarreness of the landscape...it felt like a suicide mission.

And when Number one had slipped in among them, he seemed like a foreigner, talking gibberish, as mad as a hatter, his speech slurred, and exceedingly rapid. It had taken hours to calm him down. Trumack wondered about his sanity still.

They had easily found a place to set up camp, before night fall, and all through the steaming night, under that bizarre sky, they had dug in, establishing what was to be base camp.

As soon as the sun came up, they headed out to join Number one, who had gone ahead to watch, what they thought, was the settlement. He had said the locals were housed behind a giant thorn barrier. Number one had seen only one; what appeared to be a male; a monkey type creature, much like Neanderthal man.

As they approached, they could hear the sounds of domestic animals: pigs, cows, and chickens. But, before they could attempt entry, the wind began to howl, picking up in intensity until it was even difficult to stand, leave alone remain in place. The odd thing was, the sky was still as clear as a summer day; not a cloud to be seen, one minute; then the sky opened up in a deluge, driving them back toward camp. Wisely, Trumack, decided to regroup.

The clincher was, when Number one returned from his watch post without being ordered, sprouting a fantastic story of being driven, not chased, but herded, like the animal knew what it was doing; by a tiger, no less...in the rain!

Trumack began to wonder if something supernatural had sway upon the planet.

Number one came in from outside, stripped to the waist, still covered in mud. He might as well go naked, as wet as he was. The man dropped his pants, not in the least self-conscious, and proceeded to scrub away the grime.

Trumack was disgusted!

What good is our camouflage? Nothing we have fits the colors in this place!

Aloud he gruffly declared: "We'll go buff, next time we go out. Savage and primitive! The rain isn't going to stop us! We are Special Ops!"

"Yes! Sir!"

His six men took his declaration as an order, and began to strip down.

Chapter 19

Gem was litterly, physically sick. The aggressive, perverted, sadistic thoughts of the new comers to the planet, bombarded, assaulted, and harassed her consciousness, like a hot-fire, volcanic rain, continually causing her shoulders, and neck to tense with the effort to repel them. Even Brad's mind had not been this intrusive; the Overseers had been easier to block out. But their presence had been gone more than six years before. She had lost the ability to shut so many out...

She knew even Loni was having trouble.

What of the children? How will they cope?

The filthy things the men were thinking; dreaming of lewd women, their lust lingering in daydreams, long after the awakening. It appeared also to be their verbal practice to incite anger, and competition in each other, thereby rousing themselves to greater bravery.

When first becoming aware of them, if Gem had not been on her knees to begin with, she would have been forced to go there, so heavy did the burden weigh on her. Her body shook, and trembled visibly, at her effort to shield all her brood from the madness.

She gathered all the children within the animal compound, under the excuse, Scar needed extra help feeding and caring for new livestock. Gem thought this was the safest physical space, and it kept them near enough to keep her mental shield over them, protecting their innocent telepathic minds.

Not since she had been thrown among the Overseers, had Gem experienced such lurid lack of mind control. In the six years following the disaster, she had gotten used to the quiet, gentle minds of Loni and E-ri; Thea's strong and inquisitive thoughts, and the milder power of the other boys. It had left her forgetful of the horrendous cruelty of human men. Even Brad was of a different sort; his mind at least, sought for self control.

Do I still have the ability to block out such things?

In the past, little Storm had been difficult; when he grew angry, he lost control. That was how they had discovered his talent.

Loni had learned to handle the boy. A man's mind knew better where to go, and Loni had more past experience, from dealing with Galar and Scar. The female in Gem found personal slight too easily, and...it was hard to over look furious character judgments aimed her way.

If they hadn't started his training when Storm was so young, he might indeed, be a detriment now, rather than a benefit.

But...these men were so unbridled, it litterly took her breath away; made her weep.

Little Lee squatted beside her, where she pretended to search for eggs in the grass, though her hands were seldom obeying her unconscious orders.

"Momma?" He peered into her face with a worried frown. "Why are you crying?"

Gem sighed raggedly, and quickly swept her hand across her cheek.

"I protect you..." she barely managed to return.

"From the bad, evil men! Their awful thoughts?"

So, I'm not doing such a good job, after all?

Gem nodded.

"We see how to do it..." Thea broke in, and E-ri nodded agreement.

"Let us shield ourselves, Momma," offered Peek.

"You have no idea...what they can provoke in you..."

"Evil," supplied E-ri, knowingly. "But, Momma, you have trained us well. We must practice handling it. We CAN fight it! We will help each other. Negative! Delete!" he declared forcefully.

Gem chuckled at their innocent trust, yet disagreed.

"There are many minds..."

"We should kill them!" exploded Storm, viciously, aloud. "One by one!"

"See? Already Storm is affected," Gem observed sadly, also going verbal. "How easily, it starts. Have I taught you nothing? All creatures deserve a life; even those with whom we disagree."

Gently, E-ri repeated: "Negative! Delete!"

Storm moaned softly, and contritely went silent.

As she went again into mind-talk, Gem did not notice, as a tear slid down her cheek.

"Choose, always, to stay good! Don't be like..."

"Overseers!" the young ones chorused as one, finishing the thought. Even Nitha stuttered it aloud.

Willow had sat listening. Her education still new, and developing, yet somehow, she was far wiser in this matter of the cruelty of the human condition.

That fact alone, caused Gem to weep the more.

This is why I need to protect my young!

It bothered her greatly, that at this early age, Willow was so experienced; her wisdom beyond her years.

The other children curious, turned to Willow wonderingly, and without thinking, began to probe her memories for information. The girl, of course, was not yet proficient in her defense.

"Don't!" Gem warned, quickly. "Don't be nosy. It isn't nice to invade privacy."

As a reflex, each child shut down within their own minds.

"Good!" Gem approved. "Shields up at all times!"

And so it started; the children began learning to protect and defend themselves against the outside, adult world.

It immediately eased the tension for Gem. Except for Willow and Nitha, whom she must still monitor, as they were less proficient, the others now, did well on their own.

"Okay," Gem declared. "Momma Jewel is doing all the work...animals to feed; stalls to muck; eggs to gather..."

"Watch out for snakes, and...hair worms," Willow warned, softly shuddering.

****

Possession is one tenth of the law! We were here first!

Trumack didn't believe any law existed here. He was the law, now, and the barn animals, they heard behind the thorn barrier, were going to be his! All he needed was to grab their keeper and make it known!

It was with this in mind, the squadron leader, and his men, went hunting. The rain had never been a handicap!

Chapter 20

He wasn't that smart; the monkey man they watched! There had to be others. Yet, the creature always travelled the paths alone.

As they watched, Trumack knew there had to be others. He could feel the eyes on his back, but never determined their whereabouts.

And, the soldier in him knew, this huge barrier could not be built by one man alone. The barricade wasn't natural; thorn vines never grew in such an even formation.

It was over twelve feet tall, went on for acres; a circle enclosing...what? There was a six foot door on this side...they had seen the ape man open it, and proceed to the shore of the ocean.

Not to mention the Cannery Quonset, to which the path had led...that was definitely man made!

This guy looks too stupid to think of such things on his own!

From years of erosion, and the spreading windblown seed, grass covered the side like a rocky hill. They watched as the creature opened the disguised door. One minute, it was the stony hillside; then, that vanished with a touch on a rock, to reveal beneath, an iron door beyond. It squeaked noisily when the being opened it, and slammed shut when he went in.

No! This Neanderthal couldn't come up with such technology!

It was time to catch this monkey man! To get the low down on this place...and, find out where the rest of these aliens were.

When the stooped creature left the fishery, bearing his loaded basket on his back, Trumack assigned Number Six to stay behind, and guard the place.

The rest followed after the unaware worker.

It hadn't surprised Trumack, to find no rain beyond the camp, when they left it. This place was weird; why shouldn't the weather patterns be crazy, as well? The disconcerting thing, however, was the clear hot sky above the trees...except over their camp.

What is with that?

It bugged Trumack no end, that their camouflage gear was useless. They stood out like neon lights in it! Who would have thought, the trees would have been these weird fall colors; green and black even showed up against the purple hued tree trunks.

They had put so much planning into their preparation, it was annoying to be unable to use anything. Not knowing what kind of terrain was on the other side, they had brought along for both desert, and jungle gear, but after shoving the packed trunks through, and following after, neither wear had been appropriate.

They had been so psyched to enter a different reality; prepared to improvise, but this world was beyond their wildest dreams. The surreal up-side-down trees, stars aligned in circles around the planet; nothing to orient by...and two moons! No wonder they couldn't contact Earth in the normal way, or go back there! They were at the mercy of that Portal...and it only went one way.

And, it was so bloody hot here! The only thing they could do, was compromise, going naked except for a g-string; smearing their deeply tanned skins with mud, to blend into their wild surroundings.

Even here, on the plains, they were hard pressed to appear invisible. The six remaining men slunk along, close to the ground, noiselessly. Rather than to continue following after the fisherman, they chose to return to camp for the time being. The idea of seafood had brought to mind lunch.

****

Naked as the day they were born, the assortment of men stepped from beneath the flap of the camouflaged tent, into the open. This time, they wore only a bandolier, diagonally across their chests, containing multiple small pellets, a belt around their waist, from which suspended a holster, a large pistol, and a huge knife. No other garment! Each man also carried an automatic rifle. It appeared, they were off to start a war...in their birthday suits.

Storm and Peek watched from a distance, perched in the crotch of a tree for concealment. It was the fourth day since the strangers' arrival; the boys had finally been allowed to return to their watch, Gem and Loni now confident, they could hold their mental protection on their own.

"Puft!" exclaimed Peek in mind-talk, with considerable disgust. "They are sure ugly!" After a moment, he added: "Loni is not so..."

"Big?" finished Storm in agreement. "Even I do not have hair...down there."

"E-ri is coming nine," Peek supplied. "His fuzz is just beginning...it is white. Loni says, it's to cover our manhood..."

Storm grunted aloud, wrinkling up his nose. "Theirs is most unsightly! Don't want my manhood to look like that!"

"If that is what I'll look like...don't want...MY manhood, at all," agreed Peek.

After a time, Storm wondered: "What are they doing out in that field? You can see further than I..."

But Peek failed to answer; his mind was already assessing a new situation.

"We need to destroy the pile under that tarp...that is additional weapons..."

Storm nodded, agreeing. "Need to talk to Poppa Loni...E-ri?" he projected. "Tell Poppa, they have left the compound. The rain hasn't stopped them."

A message came back quickly, relayed through the eight year old: "Poppa says, cease the bad weather. Let them do what they want; go where they will. You, watch them only, but stay together, and DO NOT interfere with them! Make no contact!"

"What if they try to hurt us?" asked Peek.

"Defend only!"

Chapter 21

Storm wanted a closer look; he swung into another tree, and away.

But, for the moment, Peek remained where he was. His eye sight was better; that was why, they had named him Peek. When younger, he'd been able to see things others couldn't; as if he'd peeked where he shouldn't.

The bigger boy's shift of position was noted by another. Out of the corner of his eye Number one saw leaves move.

Without conscious thought, as if in one movement, the soldier pivoted; raising his weapon; firing a volley. Frightening lead pellets sped toward the spot, where he'd last seen movement.

Unprepared, caught off guard, the small black boy sat frozen, like a roosting bird. More than one of the rapid-fire projectiles grazed the tiny person; one entered his chest, another the face. Then, in slow motion, it seemed, Peek plummeted toward the ground.

"I hit something!" yelled Number one, triumphantly, and took off toward the downed victim.

****

Five year old Storm was often a seething kettle. When his wrath or fear was aroused, there was little to hold him back.

One thing that often touched him off, was if someone brought to his attention the fact, that he was the only one who resembled Scar. In his worst nightmares, he dreamed the crude, dreaded farm manager had fathered him, but when it had been explained, how impossible that was...as Scar had no such apparatus, the boy's dreams had taken a different turn. When angry, Storm fantasized Scar's dead other half, Galar, had been the creator of his genetic makeup.

Who was to say, it wasn't true? His father was an unknown...

When wrath took over, Storm turned pure Overseer, and cruelty bubbled to the surface. However, Loni had tried to teach him better ways. Yet, sometimes, when Storm didn't think things through first, he lost control, and when he lost it, Storm was deadly...and formidable.

As for small Peek; only he could hold sway over violent Storm. This little boy, among all the others, would not give aside for such behavior, and because of this, the two were fast friends, and often companions. Though Storm preferred to go it alone, mostly, especially when angry, miniature Peek could always soothe, and provoke him to laugh again.

Thus, when Storm saw Peek fall, he saw red. Not only did anxiety war in his senses, along with great dread, but fury thundered to the surface, unchecked. Hate like never before filled the boy; disgust for the thoughtless Number One, and his weapon of destruction.

The reaction was quick and without reasoning; pure reflex, and Storm was at his deadliest. He wanted to kill! Storm went for revenge, thinking Peek dead.

From the tree to which he had swung to get closer, Storm opened his arms, and in a capture motion, he brought both hands together, as if gathering leaves, folding in energy. With a second motion, taking no more than an instant, as if throwing a baseball, Storm pitched a lightning bolt toward his evil adversary.

But, somehow it was deflected by a tree branch, hit the back of the soldier's head, instead of his heart, and the slayer missive lost some of its lethal effect. Yet, still, it was deadly enough to do considerable damage.

The smell of sulfur, and burning flesh, hung in the air. Number one dropped, eagle spread, on his back, in a circle of burning grass. If the gun he held, had also discharged, the man would have ceased to exist. But, by some miracle, he still lived.

The fact that something...God, or call it fate, if you wish, had prevented him from killing another, brought the irate boy up short. With a gasp, Storm came to his senses, realizing in horror what he'd done, and in that split second, resolved, never again, to let his temper rule, and with this came the courage, to admit he was out of his depth, and to reach out for help.

If the Maker can save the enemy, maybe...Peek still lives? And possibly...Gem...or even Loni, can heal my friend?

"E-ri!" screamed the boy in mind-talk. "Peek is down! Hurt! Come quick!"

****

As the lightning bolt struck the running man with a mighty force, it sparked in the air, and all hell broke loose. Number One flew through the air, flipped, and landed spread-eagle, face up, on his back, his face blacken with soot, his body blistering and bubbling.

"Holy Crap!" exclaimed Trumack. "Where the hell did that come from?"

No one expected Number One to rise again...but he did. After a minute, like a zombie, the battered man sat up.

****

Storm missed what the men did next. He was distracted by the arrival of E-ri, down at ground level, beneath the tree where Peek had fallen.

E-ri scooped up the small injured form, and just before he jumped with Peek, he fired a command back at Storm.

"Poppa says to come home!"

Storm obeyed, reluctantly, and dreading, expecting the worst: perhaps the death of his friend, and even punishment, for using such power to harm. He crept silently away, through the trees. The evil soldiers never saw; they were too busy with their own injured.

****

Storm paced, prowling like a panther, almost as an expectant father, walking the boards of the catwalk outside the central dome. Inside Loni and Gem were attempting the healing of Peek.

He had multiple injuries, some scrapes, and near misses; others, much worse. One bullet had barely missed his heart; another, had pierced the nasal cavity, and now sat between the roof of his mouth and the brain, just even with the right cheek bone, pinching the nerve, numbing the side of his face, all the way to the chin, up half the nose, and closing half the right eye. It had bruised the brain...there was worry, that he would not regain balance enough to navigate the trees again.

But if anyone could heal the brain, Gem could, and they all knew, she would give her life for any one of them.

Storm blamed himself.

If I hadn't moved; if I had not stopped to take revenge; if I'd called E-ri sooner; they would have gotten to Peek right away...if; if...

Suddenly, Thea was there pacing beside him, her soothing presence, comforting; her words soft in his mind. When she stopped him, and wrapped her arms around him, Storm, the valiant, stoic, loner, folded against her, and sank, with her, to the boards of the bridge, leading through the upper trees.

"My fault...all my fault," he muttered, hopelessly. "And Thea," he shivered. "I lost my temper. I killed the beast human!"

"No! You didn't," she comforted in mind-talk. "That human's too strong to die easily; too stupid to stay down. And why," she added, almost venomously. "I can't fathom, but...the Maker spared his life...maybe...so, you wouldn't feel such guilt."

"Me? I will remember this day, should I live to be a hundred..."

Thea softly smiled.

"A lesson...perhaps?" she offered.

But the thought only caused the young boy, that tough, fearless, heartless, Overseer's child, to break down completely. The violent Storm, just a child learning a hard lesson, wept pitiably, in the arms of his sister/friend while she stroked his back...like the mother she was learning to be.

Chapter 22

Scar poured the pail of slops into the pig trough; the squealing pigs all hurry, fighting to get there first.

Why do I always have to do everything alone lately? Ever since Peek got hurt, they've left me to do all the work alone. Not fair! I need help with these chores!

He turned, and almost ran face forward into a naked man. Scar knew he was in trouble, without conscious thought, so...he turned away, quickly, tossed the empty bucket flying, and ran.

But he didn't get far.

The butt end of the rifle made brutal contact with the back of his head...and the aggressive farm manager knew no more.

****

"Tie him up good!" ordered Trumack. "Then set the animals loose."

Number Three frowned. He wasn't one to question his leader, but weren't the animals the reason they'd broken in?

"Why?" he asked.

"Easier to find the others, if they're out chasing after their stock."

Three grinned approval, and nodded his agreement.

Number One, his face still raw, mottled black and red; his body blistered from the burns he'd received in his encounter with the lightning, sniffed the air, contemptuously.

"Powerful odor on this one! Smells like a bloody stockyard."

The man appeared none the worse for his brush with death two days previous, in fact, though he walked stiffly, favoring his burns, his swagger was more arrogant then in the past.

"We take this pig to the tent?" he asked. "Before others show up?"

Trumack agreed with a slight nod, his eyes roving about, watching for the enemy. The soldiers slunk away silently, after opening gates, and setting free chickens, pigs, rabbits...all the smaller animals.

****

"The children are not safe alone!" Loni argued, as he paced back and forth in anxious concern. "From now on, an adult must be with them at all times."

"That would be fine, if it's you, or Gem." Brad pointed out. "But when it's Scar, or Jewel...or me...If we just had guns of our own..."

Loni spun on him, growling like an animal.

"So we can kill?" he fired back. "You haven't learned the peaceful nature, yet. WE do not KILL! Except...for food."

Brad went silent, knowing Loni's approach was the better...yet?

"Poppa?" E-ri interrupted, cautiously. "They've just set the small animals free..."

"What? Why? How?" Loni probed the distance with his mind-sight.

Brad didn't need to be told the validity of the statement; there wasn't a doubt in his mind. E-ri was seldom wrong.

"Stupid! Stupid humans! Don't they realize how that will attract the predators? Come on, Brad. We'll deal with it, ourselves. I'll jump you."

"That's just what they want," warned Brad. "They want to see how many there are of us; catch some of us."

"There are other ways..." Loni declared. "I will distract, while you herd."

E-ri broke in again. "Poppa, they've got Scar..."

"I know. You stay...protect the younger ones, and your Mommas. Take them into the gardens."

"If they can break into the thorn barrier, we are not safe there either..."

But Loni seemed not to have heard. He was not only highly emotional since the healing of Peek, but appeared to be slow in his reasoning, as if still exhausted, from giving of his energy.

The two men of the clan had already vanished; jumping to their task.

Gem was fast asleep on a mat, not yet recovered after her bout at healing, aware of nothing, that was going on about her. The only alternative was for the remaining adult to step in.

"Where are the soldiers, E-ri?" questioned Jewel in mind-talk, to be more quick, and efficient.

"They have gone to their camp."

"Okay...we should all be safe in the gardens, for now. Think of another place, that will be secure. We will move everything there...when the men return."

Chapter 23

Trumack still felt pissed; even more so now that they had the monkey man in their possession.

If anything enraged him more, the squadron leader couldn't think of it, at the moment. To attack one of his men, without provocation, was the ultimate insult, and after having had a chance to think it through, Trumack knew, that lightning strike had been no freak accident.

What kind of creatures are these, anyway?

Only in horror flicks had Trumack seen the likes of it; beings that could control the weather...or, at the very least...throw out lightning bolts...like Thor. But it was obvious; here, they were able to do just that.

They tried to kill my number one man! For defending us, no less! An offense, such as that, doesn't go unchallenged. Not on MY watch! They fired the first shot. THEY started this war!

The tent flap was lifted; Number Two stepped into the mess tent.

"He's conscious," he revealed.

Trumack stood up, pushed his chair back under the table, and followed his man outside.

In the center of the camp, where they'd cleared the brush, they had constructed an eight by twelve enclosed shack without windows. This would serve as both interrogation room, and the detention cell.

When they entered, their hostage was lying on the ground, on his side, hands bound behind him, feet thrust up to join them at his back, forming a tight half circle, with his belly toward his captors.

The man's eyes were open, clear and intelligent, and...filled with livid wrath.

This is no ape! If looks could kill...ha! He'll need some persuading...

Without a moment's thought, Trumack kicked him hard where the balls should have been. The shock he felt, at realizing there was nothing there, was hard to disguise, and Trumack barely managed it, turning to his Number Two, and declaring:

"Persuade it! Try a little higher."

With a malicious grin, Two obliged, his kick landing in the ape creature's mid section.

The victim doubled up, grunting in pain. Swiftly, a second brutal kick followed after, and then another, and another, until the prisoner was left retching.

****

Not since Galar, had Scar been at the mercy of anyone. Loni treated him fairly, with dignity; force wasn't in his personality. Scar always had the liberty to make his own decisions.

But these men were cruel, sadistic; like the Overseers! Scar realized that before they even struck a blow.

"Enough!" decided the leader, at last. "We'll use the board," he declared, coldly.

They spoke the verbal tongue used by captives that been taken from Earth. Scar listened to Jewel and Gem use it; even sometimes the children conversed aloud in it. They had thought he couldn't understand, but he'd picked up enough from listening quietly. Scar could only speak it brokenly, but he understood most every word. He was intelligent enough to learn any language, eventually.

He lay there recovering. The leader had stepped back, waiting, while the other went to get the board he had mentioned, giving Scar a breather. But, while the prisoner rested, his mind was not so inactive.

They can't scare me with a mere board. Just let them try. Scar is strong!

These men appeared to have no ability to mind-talk, as Loni and Gem could. That was fine by Scar; he didn't like to mind talk; he was too slow at it.

He knew, the kids could! They never missed the gist of anything.

He suspected, the telepaths conversed aloud merely for his benefit...and maybe, to help Jewel talk. It gave her comfort, and confidence, but he felt, they were being...condescending to him.

And now...her new found mate, preferred to use mind-talk, as well.

Scar's thoughts filled with hate, as he remembered that Loni had given the unattached female to the new man.

****

Two entered the door of the shack, carrying a long, wide board, and a stump of wood; One and Three filed in just behind him. Each carried other things; One, a bucket of water in each hand; Three, a coil of rope over his arm, and a canvass sack in the opposite hand.

The prisoner's eyes held defiance, which abruptly changed to uncertainty, and then, fear, as he realized, this was a new kind of torture.

The leader stepped to the far corner to give them room.

The board was placed upon the ground next to the prisoner, the stump under it, near the other end. Two of the men lifted Scar. He struggled as valiantly as he could, but they were burly, beefy men, and his efforts were of little use. He was lowered to the wide side of the plank, his head lower than his feet. The coil of rope was wrapped around upper body; the bonds cut on his ankles, and replaced by more circles of rope, until the man, and board, were inseparable, Scar was bound so tight.

Number Two made a great show of dunking, and soaking, the canvass sack, in the nearest pail of water. Then, dramatically, with Number Three's help, he pulled it over Scar's head. The wet sack felt ice cold, and fit like a glove, against eyes, nose, and mouth, cutting off his air supply.

Scar gasped for breath through the soggy cloth. He already felt, as if he were drowning. From beneath the darkness of his veil, Scar heard Number One's wicked laugh, and the leader's voice followed, with a curt comment.

"See...Monkey man...what we want is information. You tell us what we want to know...any time you want this to stop, spill your guts. Got it?"

But, Scar's only thought was to get away.

How am I supposed to talk to these men, anyway? My mouth is covered...

Suddenly, out of the pitch black space above him, frigid water began pouring swiftly down over his face. He tried to turn his head, but it was secured by rope, and he couldn't move it. He opened his mouth, like a baby bird seeking nourishment, and only made the matter worse. He sought air, but swallowed giant gulps of water, instead.

Scar had never been fond of water; hadn't even liked to bathe. He had come near to suffocating once, when Galar had held him under the shower head, because he was angry with him. So as the torrential fall began descending down upon his face, his only thought was to scream, and fight viciously.

Even the uproarious laughter of the men in the background, failed to enlighten Scar that he was only helping them create the illusion of his drowning.

Finally, when Scar was near unconscious, the leader must have given the signal to stop. The prisoner was given a chance to recover his breath. Scar gulped at the life saving air, but the form fitting mask was not removed. Out of the silence came the question:

"Where is your base camp?"

Scar had to think of an answer, and therefore hesitated. He knew, if he didn't betray Loni and the others, these men would stop at nothing; would keep on until they killed him. He tried to think of a way to side track them, by giving them an indirect answer.

"I...live...with...animals," he gasped out.

"Like Hell!" exploded the leader.

Oh, that had been a dreadful mistake!

Again, the water gushed like a flood, out of the silent blackness. He tried to raise his head; it felt as if he was under water. That was when Scar realized, the other men were holding him down.

****

When Scar came to his senses, after the third or fourth time, he was ready to tell the men most anything; lead them anywhere they ordered; obey their every whim. He was now their subservient lackey, their source of Intel for all things on planet.

He told them about the cattle pens; the orchards; the gardens...The fishery, they already knew about.

Scar admitted, there were four more adults, two women and two men, and at least, seven children, ranging in age from eight down. In Trumack's eyes, these last, did not pose a threat; he wanted to know about their abilities; their defense; their weapons.

When the ape creature insisted they had only knives, Trumack refused to buy that.

"What about the weather? Something is controlling that! They nearly killed my number One man with a lightning bolt!"

The primitive's eyes went wide in shocked surprise.

"Didn't know about that, eh?"

The creature shook his head.

"So, who did it?"

"Storm..."

"Oh, bee s!" exploded Trumack. "That was no storm. There wasn't a cloud in the sky."

Scar swallowed convulsively, but wouldn't change his story.

"Fine." Trumack finally agreed to let it go.

The thing is a primitive; it might not know the truth.

"He stays in camp here with us. Under guard. Until we finish dealing with the other adults."

Trumack could see the disappointment on the prisoner's face; he had thought they would set him free, because he had talked. Trumack laughed.

"What about the women?" cut in Number One. "They can be put to a different use..." he suggested lecherously.

Trumack nodded, grinning. "Yeah. Incentive! Just a minute." He turned to their prisoner. "One of those females yours?"

The beast's face clouded in anger; he shook his head. Trumack read jealousy, resentment, and envy on its face.

So...there's a bit of rivalry for the females here. I can use that.

"Okay. Here's the deal. You're free to have the run of the camp. No being tied up. But, you cook for us..." The creature made a disapproving grimace. "Hey, now! None of that! You have to work for your keep. Anyway, here's the low down...when we capture the women, you can have your choice of the one you want..."

The creature actually grinned.

But, Number One let out a howl of disapproval.

"No way! Why give it to him?"

"Because..."Trumack drew it out. "He's going to share her...with us! And...because she knows him, she'll be more...cooperative."

"Ah," Number One grunted, approvingly. "Sounds...absolutely...delightful."

The look on the face of their prisoner, told them, he disagreed completely. He even dared to say it aloud.

"Men...boys...will...kill...before..."

"Really?" Number One got right in his face. "We'll see about that! We got the guns, and...we already killed one, even if we didn't find the body. I know, I killed it!"

The prisoner dropped his eyes; an obvious indication of non-acceptance, which triggered Number One's vicious temper. He went for the creature, with a vengeance. Scar backed away in a crouch, his arms covering his head.

"Enough!" yelled Trumack. "Back off!"

As he walked away, Number One hissed: "I'm just biding my time, Monkey Man. Just waiting...I'll get you, eventually."

Chapter 24

Loni's mind followed every thought of the human Leader. He was totally repulsed by what he saw, and it was all he could do to stay in his thoughts, but it was the only way to understand.

Scar had betray them. He couldn't blame him. After all, the remaining twin had always felt put upon, and nothing Loni did had actually made a difference. Loni knew he couldn't bring about a rescue; Scar would have to escape on his own, so he closed his mind, with a sigh, and decided to deal with the more pressing matter, of protecting the women and children.

The animals again housed behind barriers. Loni set his mind to solve the problems. Most of all, he disliked the latest development; Trumack had divided his men to stand watch in the gardens, the orchard, and at the cattle pens. If the family wanted food, they would have to steal it. And...the invaders were heading to the tree domes to take them over, and hopefully capture the women; kill the men...

These Earth men will stop at nothing! They mean to use, or annihilate everything in their path; to take out their pleasure on the grown women...the children mean nothing to them; they are only as animals in their way. To them the small boys have no intelligence; who knows what they will do with little girls...

Loni knew, he could not let this happen.

There is only one thing to do.

It was better to move; go into deep hiding in a cave, then to let all be killed, or worse, tormented... Loni reasoned; they were no match for guns and violent aggressors, even were they to combine all their unusual powers...

Loni had made up his mind: they would run. He gave his menagerie only minutes to gather their small treasures, then, they flew through the trees, leaving everything large, they had accumulated behind, to perhaps be stolen back later, and headed to the lagoon.

Here, beneath the great waterfall, was a enormous cave; the secret hideout used by the young divers of the family. It led in behind the curtain of water, had a vent hole above; an excellent escape hatch, allowing the smoke release. Just beside the flowing river, going over the falls, this crack came out along the tree line, invisible to most, and seeming only a volcanic pressure release. Hidden by the bushes; disguised easily by the nearby steam coming off the falls, one could build a fire, and never be noticed. It was the perfect set up, and Loni had actually thought to use it before.

However, it had a drawback...it was far from any food source, and...if they were discovered by predators, they were at their mercy.

Yet, here, upon necessity, they could survive; as scavengers...going wild.

****

"Where the Hell are they?" Trumack thundered, angrily. "These units look like they haven't been lived in for months."

He turned viciously toward Scar, who ducked to a crouch, his arms over his head.

"You said this was their main den!"

Scar cowed, shivering with dread and humiliation, beneath the muscular soldier's upraised arm.

He hadn't expected this of Loni. The telepaths were too entrenched; this spot had always been home. Scar had thought they would never leave it.

But, Loni had fooled everyone. He had not only moved, he had left a mess, making it look like the buildings had been abandoned for years.

Scar trembled, as he realized, he was left responsible; would be held accountable. It looked like he had lied to protect the others.

Coward! He had to run; why should that surprise me? He never stands and fights. I hate that stupid blue skin!

Trumack, though disgusted, knew it was pointless to beat the monkey man. He turned to Number one.

"Station a man here to watch the place. They might just come back..."

As Trumack turned to go out the door, Number Three stood in his way, gazing off along the pathway of boards and railings.

"You know, sir," his man observed. "This place is set up funny..."

Trumack knew Three was an observant fellow; noticed things others did not.

"How so?"

"Well...all the walkways lead from one building to another, around and around, then just stop, up here in the trees..."

"Yeah?"

"So...they never go down. We had to climb a tree to get up here...the buildings are too high up to just drop to the ground...Can these guys fly, or something?"

Trumack turned to Scar, behind him, and panic filled their prisoner.

"Well?" growled the Leader. "What do you have to say about that? Something you're not telling us, here?"

Scar began to shake; he knew there was no point evading; he could hide the facts no longer. Still, he hesitated.

"Spit it out, man!"

Scar swallowed, convulsively, then stuttered out the words.

"They...some of them...can jump."

****

Trumack had the uncanny feeling the creature wasn't referring, litterly, to jumping from the tree. The very word aroused his suspicions.

"Jump? What do you mean by that?"

"Use...mind...power."

"Hell!" exploded Six. "He's right! Now I think of it; that's how they disappear so easily on us...why, we can't see them."

"You've experienced this?" Trumack demanded.

"Yeah. When I was alone here...A couple of times, I thought I saw a white kid in the trees, but...he was gone as suddenly. I thought I was seeing things. The leaves didn't even shake..."

"Teleportation?" wondered Trumack. "What are we dealing with here?" He turned to frown at Scar, puzzled. "This one can't do anything like that...can you? Do you know how?"

"He'd have gotten away by now," Three suggested.

The stocky Neanderthal shook his head, a blank look in his eyes.

"Of course, he can't," agreed Trumack. A moment longer, he studied their prisoner. "How do we catch them?" he demanded.

Scar shrugged.

"We shoot them!" declared One. "I already got one, remember? The day the lightning bolt got me. They are scared of our weapons; that's why they ran."

Trumack agreed. He ordered his men back to camp.

****

Scar wasn't going to contradict these men. Why tell them about the other talents among the children? It would prove entertaining to watch this battle enfold. He had a ring side seat.

Scar grinned to himself; then schooled his features to appear stupid again. That was what the soldiers expected of him.

Chapter 25

The children hunted in pairs; a girl with a boy; those with powers partnered with those not so endowed; Thea and Storm; Nitha and Peek, Lee, tagging along. E-ri took Willow.

As the odd man out, Lee would have been alone, but as it took two to guard Nitha, anyway, it worked out just fine. The boys considered her the weaker of the pack, for, as yet, she appeared to have little extrasensory power.

E-ri felt inclined to protect all of them, but somehow, Willow seemed the most vulnerable. She was still uncertain in the trees...and the prospect of encountering a hair worm, the former episode still fresh in her mind, put her in to a livid panic.

It brought about great fear flutters in his belly, whenever E-ri heard his female companion scream. He simply felt compelled to protect her...not that, he reasoned, that to be out of the ordinary. After all, he was 'the protector'.

The adults paired off, too. Loni and Gem split up, dividing, so that those with lesser abilities were safe: Loni and Jewel; Gem and Brad. And just to be even more secure, Brad now had weapons. He had made a lethal bow and arrow. A long time ago, during one of his many courses, he had become proficient, and quite deadly, with this weaponry. On his hip, suspended from a hide belt, he also had strapped, a razor sharp knife.

Each of the children, had also been furnished with a smaller version of the last implement, not that anyone expected them to take human life with it, only to defend, or use it to cut away an obstruction. It was a tool; not a weapon...executioner effective to procure meat...or for digging, and such...

****

E-ri watched attentively above, from the tree at the end of the row, as Willow crept down into the garden, a backpack strapped to her back. He would gladly have shouldered the heavy load, but he needed to be free to defend. If she got into any trouble, he would be down there in a flash, to jump her away.

Before the guard got off a round, they would have vanished.

Willow had already gotten plenty of fruit from the orchard; it was in the small sack at her front. They had visited there first, as there was no one watching that section. Peaches and plums; strawberries and cherries; E-ri had helped gather, while keeping his mind alert for anyone coming.

But, that had been easier; they could hide among the bushes, and the larger fruit was up in the trees. Here, for the vegetables, Willow had to descend to the ground, in plain view.

Willow went first to the rows of peppers, celery, and onions, then to the carrots. Peas would take too long to pick, so she avoided those. Next came a few potatoes. Digging under the stalks, like a borrowing varmint, she was silent, careful, not leaving any trace of having been there.

My little female makes a good thief!

E-ri knew instantly, why she was so good at it. She had been hiding from others all her life.

That made him a bit angry. Brad had mistreated and neglected his daughter; left her in positions where she had been forced to do things underhanded, because of her age. From what he saw in her mind, the human world was cruel to young people. They had no rights; were dependant on the whims of adults.

I won't let that happen here! I'll protect her!

126

Though E-ri resolved to keep the past behavior from reoccurring, he didn't want revenge, nor was he unforgiving. That hadn't been the way he was taught.

The sentry was about to turn around; to ease his cramped position. He had stood gazing off into the trees for what, to him, seemed like hours. E-ri warned Willow in mind-talk, and obediently, she lay down between the rows, shifting the fruit bag to the side; her near full vegetable sack beside her.

The man turned, walked along the end of the garden, then back the way he had come. All the while E-ri watched him, and his mind, to be prepared for any deadly move. The soldier seemed aware of little sound. Perhaps, the noise of the jungle deafened him to quiet movements. He never raised his gun, even at an imaginary distant threat.

At last, the man turned back to resume his unwavering stare into the tree tops; it was from here they all expected the approach to come. The sun was blinding to the guard. E-ri smiled, and favored him with a compelling suggestion.

"You are sleepy. You've been up all night. It won't hurt to close your eyes a moment. Sleep..."

Almost immediately, the man began to nod; slumber quickly overcame his resolve, and right there, still on his feet, he went to sleep, leaning on the butt of his rifle, softly snoring.

E-ri signaled Willow, it was now safe.

She rose carefully, pulled her pack along the row. It was already much too heavy for her to raise to her back.

An instant, and E-ri had jumped to her side, to stand with his back to her, eyes ever alert, on the slumbering guard. He reached for the pack.

As E-ri raised it, adjusting it to his shoulders, Willow slipped the last few beets, and a small cauliflower into it. She bent, and with her knife, sliced a cabbage from its root. As she returned her knife to her waist, the ball-like green vegetable followed the others.

E-ri's free arm circled Willow's waist. Then the two were gone; the sentry none the wiser.

At the grotto, the two heavily burdened children appeared on the diving ledge beside the falls, only to immediately disappear behind the sheen of water. Inside, they passed Loni, gazing through the water curtain; the eternal guardian. He was better at it than the garden sentry.

Jewel was just setting a giant copper kettle of water, on a metal tripod, over the white hot coals of a fire.

****

The soldier at the stockyards, thinking the gate must be opened to gain entry, had curled up against the fence, and gone to sleep. He was certain, any unusual sound would wake him, especially if the door was opened. He was situated just behind it.

He did not bargain on ingress from the tree tops.

Lee crouched in the barn doorway; summoned one of the cows to them, so Nitha could quietly milk it.

Peek hid beside the pig sty fence. He was dangerously close to the slumbering sentry.

The black boy, since his brush with death, was leery of firearms, and the first thing he did, was to carefully slip the automatic rifle, from beneath the hand of the sleeping man, send it flying, with a soft splotching sound, into the mud among the rooting pigs. If the soldier was to awaken, it now appeared, as if the scavenging animals had gotten a hold on the shoulder strap, and pulled it into their pen.

When the cow was milked, Lee traded places with Peek, his long, sharp knife in his hand, a formidable defense, he was willing to use, should the sentry wake up.

The black boy, with Nitha, went to gather as many eggs as they could find. Willow had a covered basket for just that purpose.

We need to hurry...It's getting late.

Lee was aware, the squadron leader, Trumack, would soon send a man, to scavenge for their breakfast. If Lee had his way, they would find little; a dry cow, and no eggs.

He returned his knife to its pocket, then backed away to the chicken coop. As he went by the pig pens, Lee caught up a small piglet, twisted it in his hands, breaking its neck. A soft squeak-squeal was all that was heard, then silence. He slipped the dead animal into a pack at his back.

It didn't suffer. I was quick...

By the time Lee reached the other two, Peek, in the same way, had also dispatched an older hen, that was no longer laying. The black boy passed it to Lee, who dropped the chicken in with the piglet at his back. This done, Peek took up the bladder of milk, slung it over one shoulder, and each child grabbed a hanging vine, suspended from the trees over head, and next thing, the boys, and Nitha, were above the barrier, and heading through the trees to the grotto.

****

Storm and Thea had been delegated to stay in camp. As the pickings came in, they set to work cutting up vegetables for the stew that would make the other meals. When the meat, and eggs came in, Momma Jewel, began frying eggs for their breakfast.

Half through the morning, Brad, and Momma Gem, returned. They had brought down a deer, skinned it, and cut it into pieces. Supplies coming in today were good.

Brad was becoming very proficient at finding the tamer wild game.

And at least, for today, the dinosaurs have kept their distance.

Chapter 26

When they entered the barnyard, Scar realized immediately, Loni and crew had ravaged the place, again. The farm manager knew by head count, every animal and bird. Another piglet was missing, and so were two rabbits, and...the cows were never dry, day after day, like this, normally.

"What's with these animals?" demanded Trumack. "That's the third time this week, this cow's bag is near empty."

"Might be going dry," suggested Five. "You have to breed them every once in a while. After they calf, they give fresh milk, again."

"I'm not stupid!" Trumack shot back. "My grandparents had a farm, too. And, this cow just calved. Surely, the little beast doesn't drain its mother."

Three and Five let out a unison chortle. Trumack glared resentfully at them.

"Get with it! Find us some eggs! Or you'll go back on duty, hungry."

The leader turned on Two, who had been sentry the night before.

"You been sleeping again, or what?"

"I never left; never slept...sure of it, Boss! Honest! No one came. I WAS awake!"

"Yeah, right!"

Trumack turned away, disgusted.

The soldiers had become incredibly testy of late, showing considerable disrespect to their leader. Seven men were just not enough to guard all the areas their enemy might show up. With the dome housing unit; the animal pens; the gardens, and the fishery Quonset, they were spread mighty thin, too lean to send a man to relieve another. It meant, each man was on duty all through the night with no rest.

Their leader, Trumack, allowed the group a mere two hours sleep at noon time, then he had them out and about, once more. The two soldiers not on sentry duty were forced into K.P, while Trumack, himself, guarded the prisoner, who tagged along, while the leader searched for the enemy stronghold.

The situation made for volatile short tempers, and continual violent fights, Trumack was required to break up. He was forced to constantly discipline his men, which also fueled his own irritation.

Scar knew, if this continued, there soon would be little order, or obedience, among the soldiers. But, as far as he was concerned, it was to his benefit. If they were squabbling amongst themselves, he had a better chance of escape.

And as for the food supply; that too was a bonus. These men had no time to feed the animals; they wouldn't let him do his chores. Soon the animals that couldn't feed themselves would die of starvation, penned up like this. As the stock was depleted, used by Loni and crew, or the soldiers...mostly the soldiers, who left the guts, blood, and hide just where ever they butchered, resulting in horrific living conditions. Loni's group only took small animals, understanding the need to leave adequate replacement behind. But the soldiers were both wasteful and greedy, until...the supply dwindled. Now, they had little food, unless they butchered the remaining stock. They refused to eat the garden produce, or fruit from the trees.

Now, the little food they managed to get was seldom enough to feed one grown man, let alone seven, hungry, exhausted, fighting men, plus Scar...not that they actually gave Scar much.

Mind you, Scar knew how to supplement his own diet: a rodent here; a vegetable there. Wherever his guard went,

Scar was dragged along: the garden; the fishery, or barnyard. It was easy to steal a small morsel.

Three and Five returned empty handed.

"Can't find no eggs, either," declared Five. "Them chickens are hiding them somewhere else."

"Come on! A blinking bird can out smart you now? You're all stupid! And lazy! Thought you were men? Just because you stand guard all night, shouldn't make you this useless! Find us something to eat! A fighting man needs protein!"

As the two men slunk away, Trumack fired an afterthought after them.

"Take the monkey man with you! He should know where there is something to eat."

That would be just fine! Sure, I'd show you where there's food...but you're too picky to eat fruits and vegetables!

****

Up until now, they had posted a guard at the fishery, but when it became near morning, the guard had the habit of returning to the camp early. They also never bothered to watch the trap mechanism at the back, through which the fish filtered through the Portal. And the Portal, itself, was never guarded.

Loni had collapsed the Portal in the caverns, through which Brad had arrived. It had taken all his energy, at the time. To do another, would be even harder, but it had to be done.

He hated to close this inlet; it was a pleasant source of food, one of which the soldiers took little advantage. For some reason, they forgot about, or were unfamiliar with the cooking methods, for crab and lobster; didn't relish clams; and seemed unfamiliar with what fish were edible. It had been an advantage for Loni's menagerie.

But, now, he would have to cut it off.

It will be worth the sacrifice. We don't need reinforcements coming through; no more soldiers on this side!

Chapter 27

E-ri watched with disgust through the curtain of the waterfall. Far below, the soldiers had discovered their bathing pool. They were cavorting, buff naked, in the sun-warmed water, and enjoying every minute of it. They were none too clean about it, urinating, defecating in the water, not caring if it remained pure.

And off to the side, stood the leader, and Scar, watching them.

Scar wasn't bound, but didn't seem to choose to run away. And that angered E-ri even more than the fact, the swimming hole was being violated.

He was so concentrated on the men, E-ri didn't realize, Thea had moved up beside him, until her words spoke in his head.

"They sure are show offs. Yuk! Do all other males act so...unbecoming?"

That made E-ri grin.

"Not all...only...some. There are those who think such behavior is...required."

Jewel came up behind them; put a hand on each of their shoulders.

"Come away, children," she suggested softly, in mind-talk, guiding them from before the curtain of water. "Don't watch. This is not acceptable behavior..."

As they moved back into the cavern, the men on the ground, as if sensing, they no longer had an audience, moved off into the trees, as well.

Loni was gone, and Gem and Brad were asleep. They had just returned after another kill, and were exhausted, after the butchering. The two children joined the others in the slicing, and preparing of the meat, to be laid out, for curing and drying in the sun, under the gap in the roof.

Loni went to his knees; sat back on his heels. The glowing doorway gleamed brilliantly, as if expectantly waiting for something, or someone, to pass through to this side.

This entry has to be closed; too dangerous to leave it open!

It was regrettable; the delicacies it had brought in would be missed considerably.

He willed the opening to decrease in size, but nothing happened. It would take more than the other had to break it down.

From his eyes, shot two red beams of destruction. He aimed them, until they were travelling along the outside edge, one in each direction, meeting at the top. Gradually, the edge seemed to be eaten away, the opening growing very minutely less; smaller, and smaller, by the minute. The brightness of the portal also began to gradually diminish in intensity, until it barely shimmered.

But, his efforts were too draining. He would have to rest. The hours had passed by so swiftly. After such a long period of endurance, his energy was escaping much too fast.

Loni eased back, panting, his mental hearing and sight already gone. He closed his eyes, and...appeared to sleep.

****

Number Six had kept watch patiently for days, guarding the fishery Portal, relieved only at night by Number Two. It had mostly been quiet, a boring job, and today, after so long, and no one coming, he had thought it safe to join the other men at the newly discovered bathing pool.

Returning, at last, he had expected the Quonset to be unoccupied.

The soldier stopped short, back away, stepping into the shadows again. He moved out of hearing range, touched the button on a signal device on the belt at his hip. He tapped out the prearranged signal in Morse code, the letters S.O.S.

Number Six was still shocked by what he saw. He trembled visibly; knew he had to get his emotions in order before the other men arrived, or they would surely call him coward.

He crouched down behind a pile of white, salt-like sand, to watch the blue skinned creature, seated with his back toward him, slumped, as though unconscious, or sleeping. The being faced the glowing portal, through which the men had originally arrived.

It appeared to slumber; now he watched more closely, the chest rose and fell. Except for the color of its skin, it was humanoid, with all the features of a man: eyes, nose, mouth. But then, there was the freakish scars, where the ears should have been. It sat there, arms at its sides, hands open and limp; it was on its knees, buttocks resting on the heels.

****

Loni breathed a sigh, came awake with a start.
Have to get this done!
Again, he willed the Portal to close. The red beams shot from his eyes, moving along the edges of the dimming doorway. It began to shrink.

Now, it was only the size of a small animal hole, about three feet in diameter...

****

The eyes had opened; the being had seemed to rouse; sit forward, intent on the glowing archway in the wall. Now that Number Six looked at the portal, it appeared to be much less luminous, and...smaller.

The creature seemed unaware he was no longer alone. He did not look about him, appeared oblivious of his surroundings.

When the outer door opened, bringing reinforcements, it made no move.

Perhaps, it is deaf...

The others filed in around Number Six, hiding soundlessly, and with stealth. Trumack had even dragged along the monkey man.

The portal against the wall suddenly caught everyone's attention.

****

Trumack nearly messed his pants; if he'd been wearing one, it certainly would have been in jeopardy. An audible gasp had gone up from his men. He quickly shushed them.

The unsettling evidence was not the white/blue skin of the subject, but what was happening with its eyes. Suddenly, a red laser-like beam shot for both orbs. What it did next, was even more disconcerting.

The creature aimed the deadly beams at the portal's edge; they began eating away at it...it began to shrink in size.

****

Trumack finally realized what the thing was doing.

He's closing it! Need to put a stop to this! That's our only means of communicating with home!

He motioned for his men to surround the alien. As they moved forward, the being seemed unaware they were even there.

One by one, they crept silently in a half circle around him. Every man had the same idea...and was stewing with indignation.

If that thing cuts off our way home, we'll be trapped here!

Anger coursed through each soldier, pent up resentment at being stranded here; the animosity at each other now turned against the victim, focused on the perpetrator of this vile deed being done against them.

****

Slowly the Portal decreased in size; then suddenly, it blinked out.

It is done!

Loni slumped forward; he had no energy left...for anything.

For a second, he lost consciousness...

****

They moved in silently, closing the circle; grabbed at him, before he could prepare a defense. Without a signal command from their leader, as one, they set upon the slumped over, kneeling being.

But, before they were in place, the Portal behind them had closed. It caused madness to infect them all.

****

Loni had come aware with a jerk. Sensing movement beside and behind him, he spun raising his arms in defense. For a second, his mind sight gave him vision of his attackers: the leader, Trumack, a large knife in his hand; other soldiers with rifles raised, and standing back behind them, Scar.

Loni came to one knee. But, he had no energy to defend himself.

He was at the mercy of these predators; there was no choice but to surrender.

****

"Kill him!" screamed Scar. "Kill him, quick! Before, he can use his powers."

The men had seen the ray; fear fueled their reaction. They pummeled with fists, and weapons, kicked with brutal force, vicious hatred in every blow.

"No!" yelled Trumack, to his out of control men. "Just hold him by the arms, so he can't do that jump thing. I want to question him..."

In the moments between, One and Six were obedient, but the other prisoner, Scar, took advantage of the situation, and changed the whole scenario.

"He won't talk," he cried rebelliously. "You need to kill! Or you'll be sorry..."

****

Scar saw an opportunity to seek his revenge on his clan leader. The soldiers were no longer listening to him. They were intent on holding Loni; obeying their leader. It was too late to stop what had been done, anyway.

But, Scar meant to end blue skin rule; domination of all kinds by others. His rationale, was to kill Loni.

Scar easily found a weapon of destruction. Discarded nearby, was a metal bar, broken off a no longer useful machine. He caught it up with both hands, and moved into the fracas, slipping in between Number One and Six.

With arms raised above his head, the metal bar gripped in both hands, about to land a blow...Scar was pushed aside by Number One.

Additional wrath flooded the Overseer's reason. Pent-up indignation, the humiliation of years of servitude, all rushed forward in his mind. Growling in rage, Scar swung his iron bar. The blow glanced against Number One's shoulder, and landed square across Loni's brow.

Loni went down, but not out. Suddenly livid with rage, Scar was on top of him, his purpose clearly to pulverize the man. And, the madness did not stop there.

Number One, thinking the blow that hit him, had originated with the blue skinned man, lost any resemblance to a civilized man. The soldier joined his former prisoner, and went at it tooth and nail.

As if at a signal, the other men joined in, like a pack with the mentality: a downed enemy is fair game...

Between the stalk of their guns, and the iron bar, blows rained down upon head and limbs in merciless abandonment. In minutes, the bullying pack had clubbed the victim to a pulp.

Chapter 28

The creature seemed to have no will to fight back. It had simply sat there, and took the beating, like a limp slug.

Disgusted, by the uneven battle, Trumack had been frozen into inaction. Suddenly, he realized what he had lost: the opportunity for further Intel.

The squadron leader rush forward into the fray, screaming orders to his men, while grabbing at the shoulders of their original prisoner. His men got the message, and soon, Six and One had pulled Scar from the body of the other alien, and were holding him by each arm.

"Shit! Shit!" yelled Trumack. "What the hell you do that for?"

Scar looked at the battered victim at their feet, and grinned broadly, but said nothing.

Trumack back handed him across the face.

The monkey man came back spitting blood, about to retaliate, then, thought better of it, but the glower he gave Trumack, said, there was venom in his heart.

****

Watching the unmoving blue-skin, Number One's face brightened into a malicious grin.

"Let me finish it!" he offered.

If he expected accolades for what he suggested, it was not forthcoming. Trumack spun on him angrily, spitting out venomous words.

"Damn it! What's the matter with you? You lose your sense of purpose, since you got struck by that lightning? Get the hell back to camp, the lot of you! I'll deal with you later..."

Number One was still defiant; pointed at the bloodied body on the grey cement floor.

"What about that?"

"Leave it! It's dead!" his leader hissed, then growled, barely above a whisper. "You've spoiled any chance we had to get information. Do you think monkey man here has the full info? Hey? Now, git! I don't want to see your ugly faces for the next hour! You stupid bastards!"

For a second, Number one was shocked that his leader would blame him, then the humiliation of the reprimand sunk in; anger took its place, and he vowed, someone would pay, and sooner...rather than later.

Once more, he kicked the prostrate form, then turned, and stomped away, sullenly.

****

Six grabbed the prisoner by the arm, and followed Number One. The other men silently slunk away, each man nursing a wounded pride. Trumack would deal with them later. At the moment, he was too riled to think clearly.

He gazed at the creature; its skin was now more red, with its own blood, then blue. The arms and legs were at unnatural angles, a sure sign of fractures in many places. The face was a bloody mess; nose obviously broken; the jaw, gaping open...probably broken, as well.

Trumack sighed. He was used to death, even torture and mutilation. It wasn't that he felt compassion, or empathy. No! He was angry! And not even so much at his own men, but at the loss of opportunity, and...at himself...for his lack of control over these men.

I'm getting soft! Too long away from the military order...no commander to egg me on.

He turned to leave, but just before he did, he knelt, reached down, and touched the neck of that enemy thing. He could find no pulse.

Satisfied, he had been correct in his assumption, he left the battered being, laying in a pool of his own blood, and vacated the empty Quonset.

****

The hours passed. A stark white finger jerked involuntarily; an almost inaudible moan escaped from deep inside; a barely perceptible movement expanded the chest.

Two desperate mind-talk words went out to his mate...

Help...me!

****

Gem shot to wakefulness; sat up with a gasp. She must have been thrashing around for E-ri sat against the wall nearby, watching her with trepidation.

He was too close; near enough to pick up on her dreams.

And Thea, too, was near her feet, anxiousness evident in every muscle of her tense little body. The two were so pale, and drawn, it was obvious, they had seen too much.

She had thought it merely a nightmare, and glad to escape from it, but now, with the frantic message, she couldn't ignore it. It was very real; all the horror she'd experienced through the feelings of Loni, had happened.

It took her some minutes to regain her composure. She shook still, though she tried to speak calmly.

"Storm..."

The boy moved up into her sight vision.

The other children, also, were clustered around, yet back a ways. Brad, too, had awoken, and stood with his arm around Jewel, as if reassuring her.

She didn't have time to alleviate their worries, nor to explain. Time was of the essence.

"Storm, you guard the others, and stay in here. E-ri, and Thea...you come with me."

Just before departing, she turned to Brad and Jewel.

"If we don't make it back...you are on your own...I hope you are prepared..."

"What's happened," demanded Brad, frowning.

"Later..."

Then Gem caught the hands of her two children, and jumped all three away to the fisherman's warehouse.

****

When he argued with Lydia, it was like talking to himself. He talked aloud in a whisper, because he couldn't mind-talk that fast; she talked in her head. It was a good thing he'd finally mastered mind reading, but he was still too slow at it to follow her rapid thoughts.

Brad hated when he was left out of the loop. If he knew what was going on, he could prepare better. And Lydia was no help. It appeared, she knew less than he did.

Why did only all the blue skins go off together? And...why would they, maybe, not be coming back? Are they abandoning the rest of us...out of fear?

Does it have something to do with the soldiers coming to the grotto?

"Stupid! Stupid men!" he fumed, pacing the room. "We should do away with the lot of them!"

Storm and Lee nodded heads in agreement; little Peek shook his head, adamantly. Jewel's mind went into over drive, filling with all kinds of reasons why not...so fast, it made his head spin.

And another handicap I don't need; when you argue in mind-talk, you can't even have a decent private conversation with your wife! Everyone gets into it!

As he followed his thoughts, Peek turned away in embarrassment at being caught in the act. Storm slunk away to the back of the cave to avoid further conflict. But Lee stayed between Jewel and the girls, as if he meant to protect them.

Farther angered, Brad strode to the curtain of falling water, peering through, trying to quiet his emotions.

"What the heck?" Brad mumbled to himself. "What are they doing down there, now? Where'd they get the ball..."

Jewel moved up to join him, the better to see. Her hand went to her mouth, as she gasped in shock, realizing what was going on.

"Oh, gosh. It's a head!" and as the mind-words entered unguarded minds, so did the vision of what she saw. "They are washing a...body..."

"Oh, man!" Brad exploded in a whisper.

As Lee made a step forward to follow Jewel, the man quickly prevented the boy.

"Don't! You don't need to see this."

Lee obediently remained at a distance.

"Is that...Loni?"

Both adults had now cloaked what they were seeing, but the shock of the moment still sent their thought words out. Jewel shook her head violently, refusing to believe what she was witnessing.

"Hell!" Brad gasp, horror filling his chest. "It's..."

He turned, and motioned the children back; cautioned in a whisper:

"Everyone, get to the back of the cave, and...stay as quiet as you can..."

Together the two adults backed away after the others. When Brad finally looked at the group, they were all looking at him, accusatory expressions on their faces, as if to say: 'Who's doing the talking, anyway, here?'

Brad went silent. Quietly, he took up his bow, and fitted an arrow to it, then stepped back to the curtain of water, aiming it through, at the closest of the men, across the pool.

If need be, he meant to kill the first soldier that tried to climb the hill.

****

Trumack was more than ticked at his men. Now, he thought on the matter, this could bring a lot of trouble...

That damn monkey man! Well, he'll pay!

As Trumack caught up with his men, followed along behind, through the jungle, Scar, between One and Six, struggled valiantly, dragging his feet, delaying their progress. This only increased the irate mood of both the men, and their leader.

At least, he dropped the rod, back in the warehouse. He's no longer armed. Stupid! So stupid, to drag him along to the Quonset! And...to let him pick up a weapon! Someone will pay!

Trumack finally passed his men, arriving at the camp ahead of them. The minute they were securely within the confines of base camp, he turned to face the prisoner, and the two soldiers who held him. With a vicious back handed blow, he cuffed the struggling creature a good one across the face.

Scar seemed to realize, immediately, the futility of farther resistance; went limp instead. That provoked the Number One man.

"What you want us to do with him?" he demanded, belligerently.

Trumack glared at the two, presently, most detested minions under him, but Number One didn't appear to take the hint, that he was included, so the leader gave him that point.

"Bring me a machete!"

Two disappeared inside the tool tent.

"Drop the bastard at my feet," Trumack ordered.

The prisoner was forced to his knees. At this point, Scar seemed to realized he had riled the lead man beyond appeasement. Whimpering, he attempted to crawl away.

One, grinned, he and Six stepped back, leaving the next step to Trumack. Just then, Number Two returned, with a long, wicked looking, saber-like knife.

Trumack quickly intercepted the crawling Neanderthal; stepped firmly on his back, holding him in position. When his leader motioned, and reached back behind him, Number Two handed him the machete.

Trumack raised it, two handed, above his head; reared back, and with less thought then it takes to say the words, aimed a powerful swing at the unfortunate victim. The forward momentum nearly caused the wrathful leader to lose his balance, but the swing had the desired effect.

The blade connected with the neck, and Scar's head went rolling. After a second, the severed piece came to a stop, flipped over, eyes staring, vacantly, and empty of the soul; mouth gaping in one last breath.

Number One let out a howl of approval.

"Well..." Number Three observed, quietly, in the silence that followed. "That's the end of that."

Trumack cooled; realized what he had done, and tried to redirect; save face in the situation. A commander didn't lose his control...at least not before his men.

"We'd have gotten nothing more from him, anyway," he declared coldly. "And, he was out of control..."

"So..." Number One stood staring at the headless corpse. His body language read, uncertainty, as if he feared, he might be next. "What now?"

Trumack shook himself. It was time to take control again. He stood there thinking.

"No law here," he finally stated. "Except ours...put the head on a pike...where everyone can see it..."

"Where?" questioned Six, who had been quiet through the whole thing, simply standing back, as if determining whether all had gone mad or not.

Trumack pondered.

"The swimming hole!" suggested One. "Stake our claim to it!"

"Pollute it?" Six asked, unconvinced.

"Nah," Trumack declared. "Just set it up there, so as to tell them, this world belongs to us, now. We rule!"

"Yeah!" agreed Number one. "And this is what you get, if you mess with us!"

Once again, Number Six was dubious; he shook his head in disbelief, but joined the others, as they headed to the waterfall. As an afterthought, he grabbed the dead creature by the leg, with the thought to wash the body, and give it a decent burial.

It was a good thing Scar was dead; he had never liked water.

****

Thea choked back a scream, when she saw what they had done to her poppa. He lay on his side limp, broken and bent, with a bloody pipe beside him.

"Did he even get to put up a fight?" mused E-ri.

Gem shook her head.

"He always expected an attack...bullets, not a club. He saw a knife in the hand of the leader...he expected to be cut..."

E-ri growled out his anger, sounding like a lion, as his father, Loni, often did.

"Didn't think to use his defense beam; never even realized, they were behind him."

Gem disagreed. "No. He had closed the portal...had no energy left. When they attacked, he was depleted...he was helpless..."

E-ri growled again.

"Is he too bad hurt for you to heal him, momma?" Thea ventured.

Gem knelt beside her battered mate, fondly pushed back the hair from his forehead.

"Alone...yes." she whispered. "But...together...maybe. We dare not do it here. The soldiers might return any minute."

"Can we jump him?" E-ri suggested. "All three of us together..."

Gem shook her head. "No. We need to conserve energy..."

"How, then? Walk? From here?" he demanded, appalled. "The wild animals will smell the blood, not to mention, hear us!"

"I know. I will shield us..."

E-ri shivered with dread.

What a dangerous journey we have before us...

But that was not the worst of their travail.

****

It was growing dark by the time they made it to the water's edge, carrying the improvised stretcher. The pounding, crashing, splash of the waterfall came to them from ahead, encouraging them to hurry the last few steps. They were almost safe!

Rounding the corner of the path, the first thing that jarred their senses, even before they saw the cascading water, was, what appeared to be a grisly head on a stick, grinning out of the darkness.

"Oh, gosh!" Gem gasped softly, aloud, nearly letting go the front poles of the stretcher.

Thea let out a small shriek. Then all three realized who had been beheaded.

"Retribution!" E-ri declared, almost in satisfaction. "Finally, punishment!"

"E-ri." scolded Gem. "It's wrong to take revenge...or glory in its work..."

E-ri sighed. "Sorry, momma. But...sometimes...I feel the need..."

"That is quite evident! Remember...the Maker fights for us!"

E-ri nodded, submissively.

"But...don't you think...this time...He did?"

Gem shook her head, bewildered, at a loss as to what to say.

"Maybe..." she admitted.

To the side, the foster sister, Thea, simply listened.

"Let's go," Gem suggested, after a while.

"We going to leave him like that?" wondered E-ri, as he went by, with the back end of the stretcher.

"Ummm," Gem only murmured. "Can't carry anymore..."

Chapter 29

Trumack decided his men had done good, but now, there was the matter of finding what remained of the enemy.

Where are they hiding? How come we can't see them?

From what he had seen of both creatures they had killed, there were two different breeds, one exceedingly primitive; the other exceptionally powerful. The second kind, the blue-skins, had mental powers beyond imagination. It would take not simply weapons to defeat them, but cunning. Trumack felt he was up to it; he could outwit any race!

It appeared the blue-skins used the trees to travel above their heads; the Neanderthals, the ground paths. He first set his men to placing traps for the primitives, all along the paths.

It wasn't so easy in the trees.

And, there was still the matter of finding their hideout.

Where would a race of tree beings locate? Some place high up...the tree houses were their first lair...maybe, there is another village in the tree tops...

With this thought in mind, Trumack sent his men out in pairs, eyes ever up above. And this time, two would rest while the others searched, and not just in daylight, but at night, as well.

****

"Our biggest problem is a lack of light," Gem reasoned, when Loni was as comfortably placed, as possible, on a bed of leaves and grass, at the back of the cave.

""We can build fires around you," Brad suggested, not fully understanding the need she spoke of.

"Not heat, Brad. You don't understand," Gem objected. "The light I need to heal is sun energy..."

"But...in here...how can we supply that?"

"You can't. And, if I take it from another source...like a human, it will kill them."

"So...you can use your own kind...E-ri...or Thea?"

"Yes. But they are only children..."

"I am strong, momma," E-ri cut in boastfully. "Psychic strong..."

"True...but I need you as a guide to Loni's physical. I need you to stay apart; healthy."

Disappointed, E-ri retreated into his mind, shutting out the others completely. Gem ignored his rude reaction, and let him sulk.

"And Thea?" asked Brad.

"I can use some of her energy, but it's better to use male for male. It balances me better."

"I can do, that only, momma," E-ri declared, coming back, hopefully. "Balance you..."

Gem shook her head, adamantly disagreeing.

"Only as a last resort. I need your blue print, whole!"

Tears filled the boy's eyes.

"But, poppa will die..."

"No! I will try this alone!"

"But, momma," objected E-ri. "Without sunlight, you can't heal back. Then you...will die."

"Not if I can do it bit by bit."

"Will you, at least, use me?" Thea demanded, forcefully. "I have little use...anyway...without you," she added brokenly.

Gem sighed; then nodded agreement.

"When I need energy, I will use you."

"What do you want me to do in the mean time?" Brad asked, quietly.

"Your function, now, is to protect, defend."

"I WILL kill, if I have to; you know that, don't you, Gem?"

"I know. But only, if absolutely necessary..."

Brad agreed.

Gem turned to the others.

"Jewel, this will be a long drawn out affair...the children still must be fed. You and Brad, stay inside.

The second mother nodded acknowledgement.

"We gather food, as we always have," Storm declared, determination in his tone.

"But...you be extra careful," cautioned Gem. "We won't be able to come after you, if you get into difficulty, or protect you from afar...until after we are well enough, again. This will drain even on E-ri..."

"We understand, momma," Lee declared, firmly. "We have powers, too. And Peek can see future..."

"We can defend ourselves," agreed Peek.

Gem smiled, a soft, fond, momma's smile of indulgence.

"Okay, then. I'll begin as soon as it is light."

****

"When I take from Thea, E-ri, you must take her out under the trees above the waterfall. Move her to a sunny spot to recover."

"If I jump to the tree tops, won't that be better?"

"To jump uses psychic energy. You need to physically climb out the roof..."

"Okay...I'm strong!"

Fortunately, it wasn't easy for the soldiers to get to the top of the falls to attack them. They had to first climb a path up the side of the hill, to the diving ledge, and from there, there was no more path...unless you came through the water curtain, where Brad would be standing guard.

"Storm, you guard E-ri..."

"I will cause bad weather, if they come..."

"That will defeat the purpose; hides the sun," E-ri cut in. "No, best if Lee tells the Lion pride to guard the hill."

"Good idea," Gem approved.

"What do I do if the common energy gets too low?" E-ri wondered. "What if they break through..."

"Fight only when up closer...with your knife."

As Brad listened to their plans, he knew, if those soldiers used an old army strategy, made it to the top, behind the boys, which they were likely to do...if the men knew they were up here...

"Brad!"

"Huh?"

"Under NO circumstance are you to leave your post!" Gem growled. "You are the first defense wave. Understand! You are protecting ME! I am the central energy conduit!"

"Even if a kid is in trouble?"

"Yes! It is paramount!"

"Why? I don't understand."

"Because...all the children are bound...to me."

"How?"

"Combined energy...I did it when they were young, to keep track of them, and...I couldn't undo it."

Brad blinked, disbelieving.

"But...Willow's not?"

"She's...junctioned herself."

"How the hell she do that? And...why?"

"E-ri."

"Ah...what happens if you..."

"Die?" Gem finished. "They won't conquer their grief..."

"Possibly...you can't know for sure."

"I know...I can see...future..."

"No..." moaned Brad.

"So...it is imperative; YOU do not leave your post until after the healing...understood?" Gem pleaded.

Brad nodded silently. The conversation had all taken place in mind-talk, and he was quite certain, Gem had cloaked it, but Thea, and E-ri, had, at least, understood the gravity of the situation.

****

"Okay," Gem finished.

She pulled in a stuttering breath. She hadn't told Brad everything. She had not revealed the odds against her...not even to her blue skinned children.

There was little chance this would come out well.

Loni had a severe brain injury, and when she traded his condition, transferred it to herself, she might not heal back normal; she might come back extremely defective...brain damaged. If that happened, it was possible, she would never recover...

Only sufficient sun energy would prevent that end scenario.

****

"We need to get her outside," E-ri's voice came out of the silence, from a long distance away. "If she could absorb direct sunlight, herself..."

"It's too dangerous, E-ri," Brad argued. "You'd both be out there exposed for all to see..."

"She appointed you her guardian," the boy pointed out. "You come out with us; take up position in a tree nearby, with your bow and arrow ready. Peek can be watching farther out...If we don't do this, she'll never survive!"

"It leaves Loni unprotected in the cave, and...he's not fully healed."

"We move them both," E-ri declared, forcefully. "To the top of the hill..."

"You are mad...child! Man!" Brad was silent a moment. "It just might be feasible...but, we have to leave Willow, Nitha, and Jewel, on their own...inside."

"Better that then let Momma Gem die," E-ri pointed out.

Gem wanted to added her thoughts on the matter, but her awareness faded away, with their mind-talk voices.

Chapter 30

Gem gasped awake. She was back inside, on a mat of grasses, beside Loni.

It was night time; she could tell, because the stars twinkled over head, through the crevasse in the roof.

She was feeling decidedly better, as if she had spent some time in the sun.

She sat up, gazing about her. All around her, were the sleeping forms of her children. The three girls, Nitha, Willow, and Thea, were curled in each other's arms, between Jewel, and where Gem was laying, but the boys, Peek, Lee, and Storm, were off in a far corner, side by side, in exhausted sleep.

E-ri lay between Loni and Gem.

Always my protector. My little guardian! More like a man every day...

She raised her eyes to the water curtain, at the outer cave entrance, where she found Brad, still endeavoring to stand guard, though nodding, asleep on his feet.

Gem rose to her feet; stepped over the eight year old boy, knelt beside Loni, checking.

All healed, except the brain injury...It's morning soon. Time to finish this!

****

"Momma, no!"

E-ri awakened with a start, fully cognizant of what his foster mother intended.

"First...eat something, momma."

Gem sighed, turning away from her man.

"Okay," she agreed.

Then everybody was awake, crawling from their corners...except for Loni, who lay still, breathing heavily in a coma-like sleep.

While the others prepared a meal, Gem lay down again, dozing off.

****

Gem was panting with the excruciating pain. Confusion flooded her consciousness.

What do I do now? What comes next? Can't remember...

"Momma...take my energy," came Thea's voice. "You don't have enough."

"I need E-ri...as guide..."

"Yes..." came his voice. "See, how the brain should be..."

Then he had her by the hands, and without trying, she was taking from him. She tried to fight it.

"No...I need the blue print," she objected.

"Not anymore, momma. It's done. Loni is perfect..."

He was giving. It wasn't supposed to be like this!

"Not you for him! Not all!"

E-ri went limp. And another voice was there; new hands.

"Mine, now, momma!" ordered Thea.

They were guiding her; ordering. She couldn't fight them off.

Too weak. I will kill them.

They were so insistent!

Thea went down.

"Me now, Gem," declared another voice.

"Not a human!" Gem rebelled.

"Yes." disagreed Willow. "Nitha and I, together!"

When did they learn that...to combine energy?

"No...it will unbalance your minds..."

****

It had all happened so rapidly. As she drifted off to sleep, Gem wondered, if she had dreamed it all.

Did the children, my fire and ice girls, actually give of their energy to heal me? Were there two or three? No, Thea was already down...it was the two sisters, who gave of their energy...but, they are human...

Did the boys also play a part? How? Balance? One circle; two girls; three boys?

Impossible!

For a few seconds, Gem lay there, gazing up through the natural skylight, pondering on the subject.

Could all seven work together?

And then, she drifted away, into a deep healing slumber...considering the possibilities.

****

Gem woke slowly. Jewel was at her side, bathing her with a damp cloth. Gem sighed with the pleasure of the sensation.

"I can...do myself," Gem objected, yet just lay there soaking it in.

They got to talking, as one ministered to the other.

"Oh, Gem," Jewel revealed. "I was so afraid..."

Gem nodded against her pillow, the dry leaves beneath her head, crackling.

"The children all went down, after they healed you; dropped as one, as if lightning had struck the lot of them. You should have seen the brave little things...each giving of their energy. It made me terrified. And, all Brad, and I could do, was watch...

"Little Peek still limps a bit...his brain's a little slower to mend..."

That worried Gem.

"He's such a trooper..." Jewel went on.

"Where's Brad," wondered Gem.

"Oh. I made him lay down to sleep. The man is exhausted. I told him, I'd take over for a while..."

"How did the children heal back?"

"Brad, and I took each one out into the sun for a few hours...like they did with you...and Loni.'

"Who acted guardian?"

"I think, somehow, Loni has been protecting all of us in his sleep..."

"You're joking..."

"He's still asleep..."

"But...what of the wild animals?"

"As soon as Lee was able, he ordered his animal friends to stay away, surround us, and protect. We haven't had any trouble..."

Gem chuckled.

"That's my Lee!"

"Want some soup? It's cooking on the coals. It will take you a while to get your physical strength back."

"Okay. We'll all need time to recover. Rest and good food, will bring us back to normal...in time."

Chapter 31

The days flew by, while all were recuperating. Gem and Loni took the longest, constantly sleeping; E-ri and Thea, mostly, seemed lethargic, unable to do much.

Peek kept them appraised of the soldiers' where a-bouts. The men ranged far and wide, searching for an unseen enemy, no longer guarding the gardens, or orchards, leaving the cattle to fend for themselves, which made scavenging much easier, for the children with the energy to go steal it.

However, after a month, there was no more fresh meat, for that was all the aggressive men would eat. They had butchered, leaving entrails, and blood, everywhere, causing disease, bringing dangerous insects that cleaned the carcasses, making the farm a hazardous place, an area of disarray. Soon, it was pointless to even return there, as the animals that remained, were all dead.

That meant no more milk; no eggs; no tame protein of any kind. They took to robbing bird nests; catching wild rabbits, and digging up wild roots. Soon, the gardens and fruit trees were also yielding less, as they could not replant. There simply were not enough able bodies; nor safe moments to do that.

Brad worried, how they would feed the young ones, until the blue-skinned race was well enough to protect them.

Finally, he was forced to go out hunting. He felt, he couldn't take all the children with him, so he took only his blood daughter. Brad thought this the most logical; Willow had always worked well with him before.

Leaving the four ailing, sleeping; the boys, and Nitha, with Jewel, Brad and his girl fled through the trees.

Soon, they found a family of moose with two calves. He easily brought down one of the calves, with an arrow to the heart. The moose male, and cow fled, with their other young offspring.

It was while they were skinning, and carving the dead animal, that disaster struck. Brad had been lax, concentrating more on his kill, then alert to danger. Number Three and Four came silently from behind.

The first Brad realized the men were there, was when Three grabbed Willow around her waist from behind, and spoke. Brad looked up to see his daughter struggling, fighting with all her might, trying to bite the hand over her mouth. The man, who held her lithe body against his crotch, was laughing delightedly.

"Ooo eee! Lookie, what I found, Four. Won't we have fun with this one?"

Immediately aware, there was a second man, Brad tried to turn, but it was already too late. Four beamed him on the back of the head, with the butt end of his rifle, and blackness quickly descended.

****

When Brad came to, the world around him was icy cold, and his body felt like it was pulverized meat. First thing he did, was call out for Willow.

Seconds later, she stood beside him, appearing unharmed, with the strangest look on her face, a mask of disbelief. She crouched down beside him, reached out to touch him, as if she doubted her eyes, and was surprised to see he lived.

Why do I feel like someone beat the crap out of me?

"Because, that's what they did, Dad," Willow answered, reading his thought. "I couldn't watch anymore. The one holding me...switched places...they kicked, and pounded with the gun butt..."

Brad was glad he remembered none of that, but he sure was feeling it now. Willow went on, getting it all out, in broken sentences, trembling all the while.

"I...froze them. I think," she added. "First the one holding me turned to an icicle..."

"You...what?"

"Look...daddy..." she answered in an awed voice, catching up a dead branch lying nearby.

She held it in her hand, staring at it, until it turned white, starting at her hand, and moving outward, toward both ends. It WAS freezing, as if it were a thousand below zero out. Then the thing just disintegrated to powder in her fingers.

Brad sat up, forgetting his hurts and bruises, shocked into numbness.

"You...did THAT...to those men! How?

"I've changed...while living here..." Tears began to flow down pallid cheeks, as she tried desperately to excuse what she had done. "I got so afraid...he was touching me; the other, killing you...It just happened!" she wailed.

"What...happened?" probed Brad, knowing the result with the branch, fearful of her answer, yet, needing to know.

"The one was holding me..." she began, again. "The other, beating you. Suddenly, I just felt so terrified. The fear came like a cold wind...next thing...the man holding me was a frozen statue. The ice spread...across...to the other guy pounding on you. But...but, when it got to you, I screamed, 'No!' And, that's when I learned, I was the one doing it, and...I managed to control it."

"Oh, God! Oh, God. What have I created?"

Brad inched away from his daughter, appalled.

Willow began to whimper, pathetically; tears of denial dripping down her cheeks. For her father to be fearful at her power, was the ultimate, crushing defeat.

"No!" yelled Brad, reading the hopelessness she was heading for. "No! no...no. I love you! No matter...what you do...or are! Understand? I'll always love you..."

She pulled in a sob; and came alive in hope. In a small voice, she offered a justification: "I didn't kill them...I put them there...in the sun." She pointed to a sunny patch of open ground, nearby, under the trees. "To thaw out..."

Brad let go the breath he hadn't known he was holding, rose with difficulty, went to his daughter, and folded her in a great bear hug, against his chest. She went limp, all the fight escaping, and he knew, this was something, he couldn't afford to hold judgment against.

How come, when the others had a power, it was a talent, yet now, that it was his own daughter, he found it so hard to accept?

I'm a blithering hypocrite!

He cast the thought aside, determined to support her, fear or no fear.

Finally, he moved back, suddenly, realizing the precarious position they were in.

"We'd better get out of here...before they...ah...whatever happens."

"What about the meat? We shouldn't go back empty handed..."

"True. Okay. But, we need to hurry. If they wake up, you can freeze them again, can't you?"

Willow grinned, sheepishly.

"I can control it, now," she agreed.

When the pair got back to the cave, most of the others were asleep, and rather than wake Loni or Gem, Brad simply kept his daughter's new talent to himself, for the time being.

Chapter 32

Ever since the healing of Momma Gem, five year old Nitha had felt out of sorts. While others slept, she lay awake, hashing over things, that before, had caused little concern to the mind of a child: the arrival of a new father, and half sister; Nitha's place in the family, because of it; the appearance of the beastly soldier men; then, the near death of Poppa Loni...and Momma Gem's downward slide into un-wellness. Now, lastly, the severe beating of her new father, Brad.

He went around hobbling, his movements careful, radiating pain with every sound.

It was like it had been, when first Poppa Loni was hurt; everyone was grieving, or feeling hopeless, and lethargic, but this, was not quite the same. This pain and suffering affected Nitha more personally, upsetting her world again, turning it upside down. Why was it happening, again...and again...and again?

It made her so mad! She wasn't simply sulking, now; it was like she couldn't put away an insult, but...who, or what, had done that affront?

Nitha had no idea why she felt so angry. It was as though her brain was in a fog, unbalanced, for no reason. She had the weird sensation, she no longer had a shield, and in fact, that truly was the case, as Gem had mentally boosted the child's shield all her life.

Since Gem was recovering, Nitha was now on her own, feeling not only her own confused emotions, but those of others, as well.

All their lives, the blue-skinned leaders had sheltered the children, shielded, and protected them. Loni, the boys; Gem, the girls. And, Nitha had been like the baby of the group, because of her speech impediment.

E-ri protected her; Thea had the words for her, without Nitha ever having to speak aloud.

Then, when Willow came along, she, too, had treated Nitha as the junior sister she actually was. And Willow had been added under the family security umbrella. Accepted willingly.

At first, Nitha had felt no jealousy; in fact, it was the exact opposite; Nitha treasured her new sister. But now, it was different. In Nitha's eyes, Willow had failed in her duty.

You protect those you love; Poppa Brad came away badly hurt!

Even though her new Poppa was as useless as a stick, when it came to mental things: he could barely transmit, leave alone read, he was the first Poppa she could remember, and because, he couldn't protect himself, Nitha felt, his children were responsible for keeping him safe.

You take care of those you love!

Willow had fallen from the pedestal, upon which Nitha had placed her.

To add to this twisted reasoning, there was no one to set her straight. Loni and Gem were down, E-ri, because he was needed elsewhere, was lacking in his usual guardianship, and Thea's attention, also, was on her mother.

Nitha had become entirely too dependent on mind-talk; she could not communicate aloud without Thea.

And just when she'd become confident in Brad, he had become a distracted, hobbling elder, most times, asleep, like all the others.

To Nitha's reckoning, she was deserted by all, and like a spoiled infant, she fumed...

All her protectors were incapacitated. She felt defenseless, forsaken; abandoned.

She had to find a scapegoat; someone, who was the reason all this was happening. And then she knew whom to blame!

It's all because of those bad soldier men! Everybody thinks me useless...but I'll show them! I'll make those horrid men go away! Then, things will get back to normal!

She rationalized: Storm, and Lee, and Peek, never watched her, anymore. She could easily slip away...

Everybody is always sleeping...and Momma Jewel is either cooking, or resting, too...

Nitha, the favored baby of the family, decided to steal away, while everyone else was still asleep, the second morning after Brad's fateful, last hunt...

As she descended the path to the pool, the sleep deprived child was almost in a sleepwalking trance. At first, Nitha travelled the well worn paths of the forest, but as she kept setting off traps, the near misses startling her into wakefulness, each time. In wrathful indignation, she finally took to the trees, above.

Before she realized how far she had come, she was swinging into a tree just above the camp of the invaders.

Nitha shuddered, when she looked down upon them, observed the naked males lolling in the shade of the camouflaged tent. They were much bigger than she had envisioned.

Why can't they cover up? They look so ugly!

Before she could change her mind, she dropped into the midst of the two beastly males.

"I...hate...you!" hissed Nitha, in a venomous whisper, then switched to mind-talk, projecting hard, hoping to get past their thick skulls. She didn't care if it hurt them, just as long as they understood SHE WAS MAD!

****

Storm sat up suddenly, abruptly alert. He had sensed more than seen, danger; realizing, Nitha was no longer in the cave with the others. He reached over, grabbed Lee, who was sleeping beside him, shaking him violently. The urgent motion aroused Peek, as well. Willow, too, stirred, sitting up groggily, giving the appearance of missing an attached limb, and feeling uncomfortable without it.

Peek immediately understood what was bothering Storm, and began searching with his mind-sight for the missing girl.

"Willow," Lee began, in mind-talk. "Where is Nitha?"

He was silenced by a raised hand, asking for silence.

Then, all were viewing what the sister felt, and witnessed; confused images; flashes; flying by at such rapidity, most could not follow.

"Peek...can you see better?" challenged Storm, silently.

Since he'd been injured, and had come near death; from the time he'd been healed by Gem, the little black boy had a unique connection to the blue-skinned telepaths; his power enhanced, because of it. Though the one side of his face still drooped, the eye lid half closed, his mind-sight was now phenomenal, as sharp as Gem's or Loni's.

Peek reached out to find the wayward sister...and found her easily.

"She's by the army camp..." he revealed, still in mind-talk.

Brad moaned, rolling over, annoyed by the disturbance of the children conversing, though he had not tried to follow their conversation.

"What are you kids doing?" he demanded, then noticing his missing stepdaughter, added: "Where is Nitha?"

Willow was the one to quickly deflect him.

"She went off by herself," she supplied, aloud. "She's a little upset..."

"Aren't we all," Brad declared in disgust. "Wait a minute...you said, 'by herself'? Any idea where she went?"

The children were hesitant, none wanting to make matters worse.

"Bad...men...camp," Jewel offered from behind them. No one had realized, they had awakened her, as well.

"What the heck she go there for?" He stood to his feet with difficulty, swayed unsteadily. "I'll have to go get her..."

"No, daddy," interjected Willow. "You are still so stiff; you can't move fast...we don't want to lose you...if they surprise you..."

"Well, you kids sure can't go..."

"You are not that quick in the trees," Lee attempted to soften his statement. "Let me go. I can use the wild animals for defense..."

Brad pondered that for a second, standing there, unsteady. He really didn't relish swinging through the tree tops, chasing after a distraught little girl.

"Okay..." he agreed, finally. "But, maybe, two should go...get her back here...safely."

Willow stood to follow Lee.

"Oh, no!" Brad contested. "Not you!"

"Yes!" Willow declared forcefully. "I feel what she feels. I can track her better."

Brad wilted. On one hand, he feared losing her; the other, she was the best choice.

"I will tell you what is going on, Poppa Brad," Peek offered, in appeasement, hesitatingly agreeing with the others. "It will go okay," he reassured.

"Don't like it," grumbled Brad, certain he would lose both daughters, the way things were going. "But...guess, we have no choice..." Under his breath, he scolded himself. "Listening to the advice of kids, no less. Smart, aren't you?"

Jewel grinned to herself. "Wiser than most leaders," she comforted in mind-talk.

He grunted, disparagingly. "Go, then!" he hissed at Lee and Willow, and sat back down on his leaf and straw mat.

****

It was just beginning, as Lee and Willow arrived in the tree over head. Tiny Nitha stood, hands on her hips, before the mighty soldier leader, Trumack, and his sidekick, Number One.

Trumack angrily grabbed the child's arm.

"Stupid little pest!" he growled in her face. "Your time is over. Hear! This world's not yours, anymore. We've already killed two of your leaders, and beaten the crap out of the third. Just wait 'till we get at the women..."

But the tiny little, black haired, girl was not intimidated; at least, if she was, she didn't let on.

Trumack shook her until her teeth chattered, but when he stopped, she still was defiant.

"You'll pay for what you've done! You don't touch my daddy!" she screamed venomously, in mind-talk. "I wish...I wish...you were GONE from this world!"

Next to Lee, in the tree, Willow went rigid, gasping in a ragged breath, as if her wind had been cut off. She swayed unsteadily, and Lee reached out to prevent a fall, but she quickly cautioned him in mind-talk.

"Don't touch me, Lee! Nitha's made some sort of connection with me, to increase her energy," she warned. "You might be drawn in, as well, if we are linked."

Lee inched away, understanding. It was always possible for new mind powers to develop, and at best, upon first appearance, they could be unpredictable. He turned to survey what was happening below.

Their interaction had taken but a moment, yet below, almost simultaneously with Nitha's blistering words, the air surrounding the two men, and miniature girl, went wavy. A cyclone-like wind came up around, before, and behind them. It began whirling counter clock wise; spinning, and howling. A small black hole opened up, just beside Number One, who stood to the right of his leader.

The opening increased, growing larger, blacker, a void so impenetrable, nothing could be seen through the opening. It went larger, wider, deeper, until it was as big as the man beside it. Under his feet, it swooped, sucked like a vacuum, and instantly, the second in command had vanished.

As if struck by the backlash, Trumack went sliding back, letting go the small, but lethal person powering the transport aperture. She stood unmoved, where he had left her; he dropped, as if struck by a club, unconscious.

The portal closed with a swoosh; the whirl wind quieted, died down, and an unnatural silence took its place.

Nitha stood there, like a conquering victor, triumphant.

It had all taken seconds. Lee gasped in shock, and awed, spoke aloud.

"She opened a portal," he whispered to Willow. "She..."

But, Willow contradicted him.

"WE...opened a portal!"

Then both Nitha, below, and Willow, in the tree, dropped in a dead faint. Lee was hard pressed to move quickly enough, to catch the one beside him, or she might have fallen from her perch, and been injured.

****

Peek shot to his feet in near panic.

"Got to go!" he declared urgently. "Come! Storm! Lee needs help!"

Both boys were moving, before Brad or Jewel could object, but the elders understood the reason; they too had seen the mind pictures.

"Bring them home safe!" Brad projected after the six year olds, as they ran from the cave. Turning to his wife, he added:"Man! Jewel...what have we created?"

She took only a moment to ponder the suggestion; then she smiled, and came back with a positive answer:

"We have...raised...warriors!" she stuttered proudly.

****

Loni was weak; Gem still recovering, as they sat in a circle, on the straw, listening to Brad, when he told the story. He first explained how his own injuries had come about; Willow and his narrow escape while hunting. But, the feat of Nitha and Willow, together, over shadowed the first.

Gem shook her head, appalled at how close each child had come, following the images, passing through the heads of the young ones present. It wasn't their behavior, nor their welfare, that bothered her most.

"I wonder..." she puzzled. "Where Nitha sent the soldier?"

"To the devil planet!" Nitha declared, defiantly. "I didn't know anywhere else..."

"And...where is that?"

"Why Earth, of course!"

Chapter 33

Trumack awoke sprawled spread eagle, on his back, arms and legs out to the side. Above him, the trees swayed with a gentle, calming breeze.

He felt hung over, something that hadn't happened in years.

Not only that; he couldn't remember how he'd gotten there.

Suddenly, obstructing his view, Number Six leaned over him.

"You smashed?" the other man wondered. Then gazing about him, added: "Where's Number One?"

It all thundered back to Trumack in a rush.

That little girl...what did she say?

Her words hadn't been out loud, but echoing, like cymbals, in his head.

Trumack sat up with difficulty, cradling his pounding temple.

"Boss? You okay?"

"Do I look okay?" he growled disagreeably. "Move back! Give me some room!"

The five men moved away, yet kept in a circle, standing back a few feet, chuckling in low tones, at his obvious predicament. Trumack studied them sullenly.

His mind felt slow, but gradually, he was remembering what had passed before.

That little she-devil tried to do away with us! Nearly got me too.

Since the killing of the blue-skin in the Quonset, because they had ceased guarding the known food sources, and gone to covering the nearby territory instead, searching specifically for the main hideout, the men had been on two-by-two patrol. Trumack had figured, after two deaths, the alien beings should be too cowed to do anything but hide.

He had never counted in the children having powers.

"Boss?" queried Six, tentatively. "You alright?"

Why have they all come back at once? Is it evening?

"What happened here?" Six puzzled, finally realizing something was wrong. "And...where IS Number One?"

Yes...where IS Number One? That is the question...

"Dammed if I know!" Trumack exploded. "Struck by lightning, again...maybe..."

He couldn't remember those last few minutes.

Six grinned indulgently. "Think you were the one struck this time, Boss. You seem a bit addled. What you do to provoke them this time?"

"I didn't..."

Trumack slowly pushed himself to his feet; stood swaying unsteadily.

"Where is the little shit?"

"Who, boss?"

"The girl!"

Six made an effort to hide an amused grin.

"No girl here..."

He looked around at the others for confirmation. Each shook his head. Two and Three shrugged exaggeratedly.

"She was human!" Trumack elaborated with indignation.

"Right." Six shook his head. "No little girl here, human or otherwise."

They don't believe me! Even after what the kid did to Three and Four...

"Little bitch...did something. The kids have powers, you know? She said, I'd pay..."

"For what?" asked Number Six.

"For what that monkey man did!" shouted Trumack, then clamped his hands to his head, as if the effort had increased his pain.

"Oh. So...this was pay back?"

"Yeah."

"Well...did she get Number One, then?"

"How should I know? If he ain't here, she must have."

"Should we look for him?"

"Are you stupid, or what? Look for them! There's more kids! I'm sure of it! She fell out the tree! Look above! Find their hideout!"

"The only place we haven't looked," Two objected, breaking in. "Is up around the falls. But, there's a lion's den up there, so we've been kinda avoiding it..."

"You cowards! Can you shoot? Your arms broke?"

"No, sir..."

"Then, get the hell moving!"

****

All were back again; it was chow time, and growing dark. They had been unsuccessful at taking the hill, so had sat down to regroup as a unit.

"I think, I know where they are, boss..." Number Six declared in a low ominous voice.

Trumack raised his eyes from his plate, questioningly, giving him unspoken permission to elaborate.

They had moved a small cook tent to the shore of the waterfall pool and were eating outside, seated on the ground.

"You see that waterfall?" Six pointed up to the noisy fall of water in the near distance. "They are not above it...maybe, they are under it? Notice how, all along the ridge, on either side, we got lions? And not just lions, but tigers, too. All together! That ain't normal. They are sure, for certain, guarding something. Their hideout is there! Got to be under the animals...the only place we can't get to..."

Trumack pondered that; finally nodded agreement. After a time, he made a decision.

"As soon as it's dark," he ordered. "Tonight. We move in from four sides. Five, you start right now. Go through the jungle, to behind the hill, climb up that way; you should get there just as the sun comes up. Try to make it sooner, if you can."

Five nodded silent acknowledgement.

"Go!" hissed Trumack. "Now!"

As the man disappeared, the leader continued.

"Three and Four, you go either side of the waterfall, climb the cliff. Take no lights. When you get to the top, drop those cats; guns blazing. Every single one of them! You hear? That will make the aliens inside, think we are coming from above and both sides. Begin now!"

Three and Four vanished into the night; quietly heading for base camp, to get the climbing gear.

That left only Two and Six with Trumack.

"Two, once it's completely dark, I want you to start up the trail on the side of that hill opposite. As much as it doesn't seem travelled...they haven't been going up and down that path. We would have seen them. Too exposed, I suppose. But, it probably leads to an entrance in behind the falls.

Two seemed to agree, so Trumack continued:

"Expect anything. When we do get behind, who knows what we will find, or what kind of weaponry they'll have to hit us with..."

"We'll break through!" declared Six with exuberant confidence. "Or die in the effort!"

"Whoever is left; meet me at the top," Trumack commanded. "Pass the word. We mow down every living creature on the hilltop...then, this world is ours!"

"Even the women?" objected Six.

"The women...and especially, the girls!" hissed Trumack, venomously. "Especially...the... little...girls! They are the deadly ones!"

Chapter 34

They sat in their usual planning circle. Loni was clearly in charge, but worried. Both he and Gem still looked rather peaked. E-ri and Thea were not much better. And everyone had that hungry look of the under nourished, harried, individual; adults and children alike.

Loni was aware of what the men below were doing, and planning. Both he and Gem were following their thoughts. It was time for counter measures. Everyone in the group knew it, without it being voiced.

Loni began with the boys.

"Storm, you go with E-ri," he decided. "E-ri, use your laser sight; cut as many slim, straight saplings, as long as possible. Then the two of you, drag them through the roof of the cave, and bring them to Brad and me. Girls, you help, once they start bringing them in."

Brad appeared puzzled, sending a questioning look toward Loni. He was even slower now, after his beating, to follow the telepaths' mind-talk instructions, and too rapid visions. So, Loni quickly switched to whispered verbal, and spelled out his plans aloud.

"You and I will build a barrier with the logs, across the water curtain opening...inter-linked, and with cross supports...like weaving a rug..."

"Ah," Brad agreed, understanding instantly. "Like you did with the thorn barrier around the farm?"

Loni nodded.

"But, are you up to such physical exercise?" Brad countered. "You are still quite unsteady... and, your psychic mind..."

"Isn't up to par to support my physical," Loni finished. "But, then, you are not so good physically, either..."

"I'll make these...stiff joints work!" Brad decided insistently. "After a while, they'll stop complaining, and I won't even notice. A little physical exercise is good for what ails me!"

Loni actually grinned, at the man's bravado. Next, he turned to Lee.

"While we are doing this, Lee, you and Peek find, at least, four or five young Hyenas. Can you control them enough so Peek can help you herd them?"

"I think so, poppa."

"Good. I want you to bring them down into the cave..."

"In here?" Brad challenged, nervously.

"It will take them a while," Loni reassured. "They must first kill bait to attract them. Feed them only enough to tempt them, Lee. They need to be hungry to attack the soldiers. By the time the boys return, get the dogs down through the roof, we should be finished putting up the barrier. Oh, and Lee..." he called after the boys, just as Peek disappeared through the ceiling opening. "Can you keep them quiet?"

Lee shook his head, dubious. "Hyenas aren't naturally silent when attacking their prey, poppa. Their laugh gives them courage...but, I'll try."

"Your best, is all I ask..."

"Don't you think?" Brad suggested. "The waterfall noise will disguise any sounds in here?"

"True," Loni agreed. As Lee disappeared, the telepath spoke to Jewel, and his mate.

"I don't know that we can take much with us, but gather, and prepare, what food we can carry. By the time morning comes, we'll all be pretty tired. Both our psychic and physical will be so drained..."

"Physical will not even be there," Gem agreed. "But, I have a plan..."

Loni seemed not to hear the mind words. He continued his musing to himself.

"Don't know where we'll end up, if we do escape..." He shook his head, for the first time, uncertain. "But, where ever we go...we all go together!"

The adults nodded agreement, determined to fight to the end. As the first stripped saplings were dragged through the aperture above, the men set to work.

****

Trumack desperately missed his Number One man; he had been one to think ahead, always coming back with feedback. But now that the leader was back to normal himself, Number Six would serve the purpose of right hand, just as well.

Trumack knew what he was up against now, and it galled him no end.

We are fighting a bunch of kids, no less! How many are there? Can't be sure...two at least. But, probably more.

Kids are a piece of cake. Yet, kids such as these? Puts the cold shivers in my skivvies!

How do you fight powers that freeze you, or send you to...hell?

He looked up to the hill top, where the lions crouched, all along the ridge, gazing down, their eyes glowing in the dark, as if saying: 'We are waiting. Come and have at us.'

Standing in relaxed attention, awaiting the signal from Two, that he had found the entrance, Trumack seethed, allowing the livid anger to course through every fiber of his camouflaged, muscular frame, yet holding it at bay, for the right moment, to fuel his future battle ready energy.

Yet, underneath, he wasn't the man he appeared.

Ever since his encounter with the irate, miniature girl, and Number One's disappearance, Trumack felt naked; exposed. He had even donned his uniform again, complete with knife, sidearm, rifle, and grenades.

When he did walk or march, he no longer struck out with confidence, but walked bow-legged, as if he were an infant with a load in his pants. The rough material felt coarse against skin that appeared to be unusually sensitive. It was as if, his hide no longer belonged to him, was foreign.

Trumack had decided; there was no way in hell, he would ever fight naked again!

Not with these alien brats!

At the leader's donning of garments again, Number Six and Two followed suit, and before they took off for their climb, Three and Four did likewise. Only Five still travelled in the buff, as the action of his commander was unknown to him.

****

After leaving their team, and reaching the cliff, Three chose the right side; while Four went to the left. Each made good time, climbing most of the night.

Toward morning, sporadic gunfire resounded from both sides. The soldiers had encountered the animals.

From the right, Four heard his comrade. Roars and screams, not all of them the angry, provoked, vicious, growls of carnivores. A human cry of fear; then one of pain...terror. The automatic spat erratically, and cut off unexpectedly, as though broken, or damaged, by some unknown means.

Four had an image of Three stepping back toward the cliff, as if the man was sending a fear plea for help. He shivered, as he heard a shriek of surprise; a cry of despair. It seemed to drop, and then fade with distance, then stop abruptly, as if a sharp knife had silenced the voice.

He suspected that Three had fallen to his death; his companion was gone. A lot of good the climbing gear had done him. The animals above, when he reached the ridge, had been a too formidable force to contend with.

Better watch my own back.

But it appeared all the defenders had gone to the right to join that pack. Four had already done away with the few remaining to finish him.

Four didn't take time to grieve; the fatality merely fueled his wrath, and filled him with a stronger purpose. As he moved through the weeds, mercilessly mowing down the large cats, that popped up their heads, he was stayed on just one purpose: He would meet up with his commander, come hell or high water!

****

When his man on the hillside path came back to inform him, there was indeed a cave behind the falls, Trumack moved over the cleared pathway, quickly. He would be the first to enter; He would lead his men to victory, at last!

But, he did not expect to find the entrance blocked. A sturdy barrier of fresh logs barred their way.

These guys are good! But kids aren't this strong. Must be some adults left...even women can't build something like this...

Trumack admired their tenacity and initiative. As he had used the night to prepare, and sneak up on them; they had been building battlements; defenses.

If these are women...Of course, they'll be smart. Figures! Look at what the kids can do.

Approval climbed into his mind set; Trumack grunted in respect.

This adversary is worth my efforts...Still...YOU WILL ALL DIE! This is my world, now!

He meant to follow where ever they went; hunt them, until the last alien was disposed of. He was stranded here, and they had to go.

There just isn't enough room for them and us!

But...maybe...I might just keep one woman for myself. The one with the brains, guiding the lot!

He chuckled at that, as he turned to his Number Two man.

"Get me a chainsaw!" he ordered coldly.

Chapter 35

The men were nearly upon them; there was no defense left.

Gem had flashed on the future, but only minutely; it was merely what might be. They had a chance to change the outcome.

But, they would have to have the sun to do it. That ultimate energy was desperately needed.

While the men had been working, Loni and Gem had carried on a mind-talk conversation, keeping Jewel and Brad in tune, as they discussed their escape. The two telepaths had decided this was the only means for saving the children; there was just nowhere else to go.

Yet, there was always the terrible chance, this wouldn't work, with their psychic state so depleted. They had deliberately kept the girls as inactive as possible, to conserve their unit force.

Brad and Jewel were doubtful, considering it too drastic, but as they witnessed the determined, hell-bent way the soldiers were coming at them, the human pair finally agreed with the plan. This was the one chance in a million, and it had to be tried...even though, it was the last place any of them wanted to go.

****

As the whine of a saw came faintly to the ears of the men inside, Loni gave the order to vacate. He ordered Lee to instruct the Hyena cubs to sit quietly while the beings with them climbed up the wall toward escape; then they were to attack anything that entered the now darkened space.

When Peek and Lee were gone, and Brad close behind, Loni followed rapidly. The adult men had been the last defense, but now the telepath was done with conflict. It was time to flee!

When they reached the clearing, Gem already had the children in place; in two inner circles. All the men need do, was join hands with their mates.

****

When the grind of the saw quieted, and the severed logs fell forward into the darkened interior, the silence was deafening. Trumack listened intently, before stepping forward, at the front of his men.

He could hear quiet breathing; then a smothered, drawn out, maniacal laugh.

What the hell is that?

And then, the half-grown pups were suddenly upon them, all five at once! But they weren't puppies, not domestic, at least. No, they were wild...Hyenas! And big!

"Oh, God! Fight for your lives!"

Trumack couldn't get the range to lift his rifle up, and fire...but Number Six and Two, behind him, could. The spatter of gun fire mowed into the lot. Trumack dropped his weapon; was fighting a medium sized animal with his bare hands.

He managed to reach his sheathed knife with one hand. In one swift motion, he cut across the throat. There was a yelp, and the young beast went limp.

Trumack gazed around the cavern. Five dogs were dead; his two men safely standing. But no enemy...other than the carnivores.

Trumack, of course, had come out a little less lucky. His clothing was in shreds; his left forearm, bleeding.

So much for not fighting in the buff!

"Find them!" he growled, angrily.

As his two men searched the dark corners of the cavern, Trumack stanched the flow of blood from the bite on his lower arm.

"No one here," Two stated expressionlessly.

"But," cut in Six. "We have a hole above, in the roof. That's how they went out."

"Find the way up, and over. After them!"

****

Gem breathed a sigh of relief, at the vision that met their anxious gaze, of the sun rising over the land. A tangerine globe above trees of mauve, rust, and caramel, the purple tree trunks; turquoise water beyond that, so clear, it reflected the whole country around...air so pure...you could find it nowhere else. Tears formed in her eyes.

What a sight! The last one we will ever see of Azure Blue. We are saying goodbye...

"Hurry," Jewel encouraged. "They are minutes away..."

Behind them, the soldiers had broken through the barrier, and were now in a battle for their lives, with the Hyena cubs. You could hear the snarls, and howls; pain filled yelps, mingling with the staccato rapid-fire echo of gun fire.

The women fled with their menagerie of children, climbing the hill top, to an open field covered in tall grasses, that had either been torn off for bedding, or flatten to the soil, by their recent occupations.

Gem shooed the children into circles; the three girls, at the center. They were the core power! The four boys, in the middle; the protection! And the mommas on the outer rim.

Loni came with Brad, just in time to join that outside circle.

The psychic powerful girls joined hands; the boys, in the middle, did the same. The outside ring, followed suit.

"Pray, boys!

"Willow, think of home!" Gem commanded. "Brad and Jewel! Think of home!

"And Loni. Follow my mind.

"Now! Nitha! Open the portal!"

In trepidation, Gem realized, only the children had vanished, but...the portal was still open, the wind howling; the dark center, shifting, as if moving from one area to another, going forward, then distant, and back again.

Where has it taken them? With it ever changing like this, is it safe to follow?

While they watched, the tunnel could lead to another planet...or even another time period.

The soldiers were struggling up the hill behind them.

We have no choice; we have to take a chance!

"Go in manually!" Gem ordered. "Think of home. Brad! Jewel!"

Then they were all speeding through space, and time. But...to where...to when?

****

Trumack got there just in time to see the last blue-skin enter the vortex. The portal was closing...

Five came over the ridge behind the hill, just as Four joined Two and Six behind their leader. Trumack yelled at his four remaining soldiers.

"Follow them in! Don't let them get away!"

Trumack made it to the opening; just as he was sucked in, the portal closed.

The four soldiers left behind were pushed back; they dropped unconscious, as if struck by lightning.

Epilogue:

The time travel aged them. E-ri knew, now, he was fourteen. Both his head, and body told him so. All knowledge was there, as if he had lived the time span between.

Even the advanced learning to function...beyond, what was needed was in his memory. It was still a different world, an unfamiliar society, and that would mean a learning curve. It would be so for all...except with Willow.

She was originally from Earth.

Willow would now be thirteen; the others twelve and eleven.

If I could just locate them...

If they were where he thought they should be? On a planet where young folks had no rights. Here they would be at the mercy of self-centered adults, bent on satisfying their own desires.

On this world, those of his age were considered inexperienced; self-absorbed; even too immature to take part in the making of important judgments or decisions. All would be painted with the same brush, even if some were decidedly different.

Not to mention the attitude toward those with paranormal powers...

He shivered with dread at the thought.

Here, he could not read minds...at least, not yet. Too many thoughts to sort through...He felt as though he were stupid...handicapped; impaired.

Where are the others? The girls...my brothers? And what happened to our parents?

Has each been sent to a different location?

###

About the Author:

If anything, Margaret Afseth is a survivor. She spent most of 2014 battling Cancer, a tumor pressing on the optic nerve. Now she counts herself among the rare few who, in her words, conquered the 'Beastie'. Though now of low vision, with the aid of her daughter to publish, she continues to write.

From an early age, she was making up stories. While raising her four children alone, she wrote her first novel...in long hand. Unfortunately, she gave the only copy of the manuscript to someone of the opinion, she should not be writing at all. He burned it.

Discouraged, she went underground, not surfacing again until her senior years, when at the age of seventy, 2013, she rewrote and published, as a three part series, the lost novel, calling it The Aopato Chronicles.

Since then, Margaret has gone on to write the Noor Chronicles, published 2014, the last book of which was written while she was undergoing Chemo and Radiation treatment.

Her present set of novels are the Deception series. These books take a good look at survival in our most imperfect world...

Margaret is a widow, with four grown children, five grandchildren, and one great grandchild. Her experience comes not from academic education, but from the great reservoir of knowledge, gained from observing human nature.

Discover other titles by Margaret Afseth Amazon.com
Aopato-book 1(Aopato Chronicles)
Remedy-book 2(Aopato Chronicles)
Turn Back-book 3(Aopato Chronicles)
Hidden From View(a short story)
Gentle Beast-book 1(Noor Chronicles)

Soul Saver-book 2(Noor Chronicles)
Healer Nest-book 3(Noor Chronicles)
Monsters Among Us-book 1(Deception Series)

If you enjoyed this book, here is a sample of book
three of the Deception Series, coming soon:

ULTIMATE RECKONING

By
Margaret Afseth

PROLOGUE:

When they thought of home, each pictured it differently. That was their first mistake. The second glitch in the method, was the portal performance. A five year old may be powerful, but when the directions are muddled, how could a small girl plan the destination; how could Nitha possibly know where the end should be? Especially, when she had never been there.

The center circle was the three girls; the next, held four boys. Surrounding them, their four parents.

Of the children, seven year old Willow was the only one who had experienced life on planet Earth; so she was their guide. When Momma Gem said, 'think of home,' she first thought of the ocean, where she had been swimming with her father, even from an extremely tender age. The boat they last sailed on, was her most recent recollected residence...

But wary, they might land in water, and not wishing to drown her friends, she rejected that memory, and so, at the last moment, opted for a long forgotten recall of her younger momma, from her baby years...

The result was, that city was where she directed her sister to take them.

However, there were other minds involved; thinking not of home, but what such a habitant might be like...

****

E-ri landed alone, with a jar, on the sand bar of a river bank. He went sliding painfully a good ten yards, to thud against a ramshackle, abandoned tool shack, coming to rest with skinned thighs, and scraped lower back. And, he was no longer wearing his animal hide shorts.

The last thing he wanted was to be buff naked. Not now, at the age of fourteen! He resolved, he would find garments, if he had to steal them!

Above, Sea gulls circled, their raucous calls resounding. E-ri looked around for the others.

Not even Willow had come along on HIS ride.

****

Peek felt strange. He was now twelve.

He opened his eyes, his face buried in gray smothering ash. When he raised it, he could still hear the far away rattle of gun fire.

For a second, he wondered, if he had been left behind.

He remembered vaguely, at the very last second, of the journey through the dark, shifting tunnel, letting go the hands nearest him. He had been trying to think of human beings with skin the color of his own. That was where he had wanted to go.

Am I still with E-ri, and Willow? No one else here...

Where are Storm and Lee? Nitha, and...Thea?

I seem to be alone...

Peek coughed hoarsely, attempting to rid his lungs of the dust in the air; gazed about him, puzzled; confused. Trying to see through...smoke?

Where am I?

There were damaged buildings in the distance; rubble and bricks all about him; a path strewn with debris: broken wooden frames; twisted metal bars sticking up out of the ground.

What is this place?

Still the rattle of weaponry; the repercussion of a explosion...

But there were no trees, nor the normal call of an animal; not even the unpleasant growl of a dangerous predator.

As Peek sat hesitant, a rough hand grabbed him from behind, and shook his shoulder. The voice that followed it, was speaking foreign words, yet the boy could understand them, by reading the thoughts behind them.

"Come, boy! You can't remain here, in the middle of a battle zone. You'll be certain to be killed. Did you lose your parents? Come along with me. I know where to go..."

Peek looked back, and up, as the man continued; he was too tired to follow the rest of his ramblings.

He rose to his feet, in the grip of the fist on his arm, following along hesitantly; stumbling at times, but the man would pull him up each time, and carry on. His benefactor wore something like a loose, dingy, grey robe, that covered most of his body; sandals on his feet, and a towel-like head covering tied with a rope. The skin that Peek could see was dark brown; the other hand held a rifle on a thin leather strap.

"We need to get you some clothing...you can't go around stripped to the skin. What's the matter with you? When you fled, why didn't you slip something on?"

If Peek hadn't been taught to read minds, he would never have picked up half the man said. The language was as unlike the speech of Azure Blue, as mind-talk was to a spoken word.

Not to mention, not once, did the man allow him a chance to answer.

Peek tried to glean where he was, from the mind of his companion. All he was able to pick up, was this was a place called...Syria.

And the soldiers, and leaders here, were trying to purge the population of malcontents...although, they appeared to not care if they killed whole families to do it.

****

"Go to a place where there are others like me!" Lee thought desperately, just before Peek let go his hand.

When he found himself in a store front window, naked on a tattered couch, Lee had the presence of mind to steal clothing.

He stepped over a ledge, into the darkened interior beyond, hearing the warning clang of an alarm in the air. He sensed what it meant; he was an intruder; he didn't belong there. The half Asian boy sped into action.

All he could find were cut off jean shorts, frayed along the bottoms. For some reason, he had grown much bigger, at least twice his original size...as if, he had aged to...twelve?

No way!

He finally found a pair that fit, and quickly, donned them. Then, as he heard the squealing of tires around the corner, Lee, again, stepped through the window, and into the street, fleeing in the opposite direction.

****

Storm tossed around in the stream of ever shifting locations. His view of the world, they were suppose to go to, muddled. He had no inkling of the area where he should end, so he simply tried to concentrate on following through the vortex. When Gem had said, 'think of home', he had little idea of where he might fit in. He had so often heard himself referred to as a Neanderthal, by the invading soldiers, he was of a mind, that he would be unwelcome, where ever he landed. Thus, when he dropped into time again, it was to arrive on the grounds of an amusement park, situated in an open field; a circus of animals and freaks.

****

Thea and Nitha came out together, still holding hands. Their idea of Willow's Earth home was a place where young girls were exploited.

They came down, thudding rather violently against dirty payment, somewhere in the red light district of an unnamed city.

Eleven now, their bodies were just budding; the curves slightly beginning to show. Before they could crawl away into the nearby ally, a slurred, drunken voice broke the silence.

"Hey! Now, what we got here? You two lost, or what?"

A trembling hand caught at Nitha's long black hair, keeping her stationary. Shocked by the cruel action, she gasped aloud, but made no other sound; too terrified to move, never having be so manhandled before.

Thea looked up, horrified, as well. Up the dirty pant legs, past a huge beer belly, to a scruffy, whiskered face on a street bum. She grabbed at her companion, ripped her free, and turned to escape, with the usual method, she used back home.

But...nothing happened.

"I can't jump," she moaned in mind-talk. "My energy is too depleted from travelling through the portal." After a moment, she added: "I can't even compel him...or even read him."

"Oh, help!" Nitha shouted, fearfully, in mind words. Only Thea could hear. "What do we do?"

"Hide!" returned Thea, desperately.

As the girls scrambled away from the man's reach, he ogled them.

"Ooee!" he chuckled, with delight. "How about that? Two bare bums; one in blue; the other pink. Got a little boy-girl color going here. I like that!"

Mortified, as realization struck, Nitha transmitted telepathically: "Oh! Gosh! Thea. We don't have a stitch on!"

"And..." Thea agreed, pulling her friend through an open cardboard box, then behind a metal dumpster. "We are no longer five. I think we are...eleven!"

Holding their collective breath, the girls sat there, trying to look smaller, awaiting the worst.

****

"What's this?" the mob boss demanded, as the wino entered, dragging two naked girls by the hair; one in each hand.

They were scrawny, under developed, and one so pale blue, it appeared, he had found her hiding in a refrigerator unit.

"You expect me to pay you for this? Why the one is so blue, she looks frozen."

"You could use her, as a special one, boss," the bum suggested.

His employer shook his head, looked to the beefy protector at his side, who grinned knowingly, but didn't speak.

"Maybe," the boss man said, considering, then shook his head a second time. "Nah. I might take the dark haired beauty...there's plenty call for one her age..." His eyes bore into Nitha, and she cringed. "What's your name, little dove?"

Nitha shook her head; she knew, the moment she opened her mouth, because she was so afraid, she would certainly stutter.

Thea spoke for her. "She can't speak..."

"What? She dumb?"

"I talk for her, and...to her."

"No! No!" shouted the seated man behind the desk, making the girls tremble in their skin. "Don't need two joined at the hips!" He shook his head again, and seemed to calm. "So...what are your names?"

"I'm Thea. This is Nitha..." Thea gestured to the darker skinned girl at her side.

"Right. Might be a nice touch," pondered the boss. "Helpless, dumb...good for the protective sort. So...we have a broken dove, and a...ghost. I'll take the silent dove...but, not the bossy sassy."

"What am I to do with the cold one?" asked the wino, hesitantly.

"Don't care," returned the boss. "Just get it out of here."

"Do I get something for the pretty one?"

The boss shrugged, thought a moment. "Give him some grub," he ordered of the pug-faced man at his side. "And, take this one." He pointed to Nitha. "And get her something pretty to wear..."

As the girls were pulled apart, Nitha to one door, Thea pushed toward the outside entrance, Thea tossed back over her shoulder, a reassurance to Nitha, in mind-talk.

"Soon as I get free, and get enough energy, I'll find you; come and jump you away from here..."

None of the men were aware, any thought words had been spoken.

"Okay," agreed the other girl, silently.

Yet, fear still remained, in both girls.

To keep reading please go to Amazon.com to purchase.